The FReNch CONFeCTION
and The GReeK who STOLe ChRISTMas

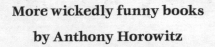

**More wickedly funny books
by Anthony Horowitz**

Granny

The Switch

Groosham Grange

Return to Groosham Grange

The Devil and His Boy

More Bloody Horowitz

The Diamond Brothers books:

The Falcon's Malteser

Public Enemy Number Two

South by South East

The Blurred Man

The French Confection

I Know What You Did Last Wednesday

The Greek who Stole Christmas

Anthony Horowitz

The FReNch CoNFeCTioN

aNd The GReeK who SToLe ChRiSTmas

A DiAMOND BROTHERS CASE

**WALKER
BOOKS**

First published individually as *The French Confection* (2002),
and *The Greek Who Stole Christmas* (2007)
by Walker Books Ltd, 87 Vauxhall Walk, London, SE11 5HJ

This edition published 2016

2 4 6 8 10 9 7 5 3 1

The French Confection © 2002 Gameslayer Ltd
The Greek Who Stole Christmas © 2007 Stormbreaker Productions Ltd
Introduction © 2007 Gameslayer Ltd
Illustrations © 2016 Tony Ross

The right of Anthony Horowitz and Tony Ross to be identified as
author and illustrator respectively of this work has been asserted by them
in accordance with the Copyright, Designs and Patents Act 1988

This book has been typeset in ITC Veljovic

Printed and bound in Great Britain by Clays Ltd, St Ives plc

British Library Cataloguing in Publication Data:
a catalogue record for this book is available from the British Library

ISBN 978-1-4063-6916-8

www.walker.co.uk

Contents

TIM DIAMOND INC.

23 THE CUTTING, CAMDEN TOWN, NW1

Dear Reader,

It's been a while since I had lunch with the chairman of Walker Books. He's an old man now. Most of his hair's gone white and the rest of it's just gone. He wears bi-focal glasses but he doesn't really need them. He's forgotten how to read. He'd forget his own name if it wasn't written on his Zimmer frame.

And yet I still remember the day he took me out – just the two of us, face to face, though with a face like his I wouldn't have bothered. We met at the poshest restaurant in London ... then crossed the road to the café on the other side. He ordered two bacon sandwiches without the bacon. He was a vegetarian. And that was when he tried to sweet-talk me into writing an introduction for this collection of stories. But it takes more than a bag of sweets to get Tim Diamond on your side, so I told Walker to take a walk.

A few days later he came tiptoeing round my flat with a bag of books: a bit like Santa Claus without the beard, the laughter or (it was the middle of June) Christmas. This was his deal. Three dozen adventures of Maisy mouse and an old Where's Wally? annual in return for a couple of pages by me. But as far as I was concerned, there was still one book missing. The Walker cheque book ... preferably autographed. Unfortunately, when I pointed this out, the chairman just scowled. That was the sort of man he was: small, hard-edged and leathery. Just like his chair.

"I need an introduction!" he cried.

"All right. How do you do, I'm Tim Diamond," I said.

"No, no, no. For the book!"

"Why do you need an introduction?" Nick – my kid brother – asked. "You probably won't sell any copies anyway."

Actually, in the end, it was Nick who talked me into writing this. He reminded me it's only thanks to Walker that I've become known as England's sharpest, most successful private eye, the sort of detective that makes Hercule Poirot look like a short Belgian with a funny moustache! I have to admit that Walker have been behind me all the way. About thirty miles behind me.

They launched this book with a slap-up dinner at the Ritz. The service was so slow, the waiters deserved to be slapped. Twelve journalists came, but only eleven left. That was how bad the food was.

At the same time, they launched a major advertising campaign ... it's amazing how much you can achieve with three toilet walls and a can of spray paint. Soon the name of Tim Daimond was everywhere. Spelling was never their strong suit. And what can I say about the new covers? They'd been specially designed to stop people noticing the new price. But it was the same old paper though and for that matter the same old stories. They were written so long ago that the Domesday Book was two ahead of them in the bestseller lists, and frankly it had better jokes.

Anyway, here's the introduction. I'm not quite sure how to begin. Introducing the introduction is always the hardest part. I'm glad I'm not a writer. And if you met the guy who does the writing for me, you'd be glad too.

His name is Anthony Horowitz – and I use him to put my adventures down on paper. Let me tell you a bit about him. A lot of people have compared him to JK Rowling. They say he's not as good. He has a wife, two sons, a stuffed dog and a word processor, and the word processor is the only one that doesn't want to leave home. You ever see "Foyle's War", "Midsomer Murders" or "Collision" on TV? Me neither – but he wrote them all. They're the only programmes people fast-forward through to see the advertisements. He also writes a lot of books. About thirty of them at the last count. Enough books to immobilise a mobile library.

I met him just after I'd cracked the case that became known as "The Falcon's Malteser". I don't think his career was doing too well just then. How many other writers tap-dance outside Harrods in their spare time? Anyway, I told him my story, he began to write – and the rest was history. Actually, nobody wanted history. They wanted an adventure. So he had to write it a second time. But it worked. "The Falcon's Malteser" sold twenty-seven copies in Waterstone's the day it was published and I only bought twenty-six of them. Soon we were right at number one in the Bookseller chart. OK – it was the remainders chart but you've got to start somewhere. "The Times" critic said the book was "hysterical" and she should know.

Since then, I've cracked more cases than the entire baggage-handling department at Heathrow Airport, and Horowitz has written them all. "Public Enemy Number

Two", "South by South East" – one day maybe he'll come up with a title that somebody actually understands. I had a pretty hairy time in Australia recently and he says that'll come out in a book too. Apparently the title is going to be: "The Radius of the Lost Shark".

Which brings me to the book you are now holding in your hand (unless you didn't buy it, in which case it's still on the shelf ... a bit like my editor). The two stories in this book all happened to me in the space of one year and all I can say is, I'm glad it wasn't a leap year. One extra day would have been the death of me.

Why do so many people want to kill me? I could have been plastered all over Paris in "The French Confection". And as for "The Greek Who Stole Christmas" ... well, next year I'm giving that particular holiday season a miss. Tinsel, turkeys and gift-wrapped hand grenades? No thanks.

You may have noticed that this edition is printed on special cheap paper and as for the glue ... all I can say is, don't leave it out in the sun. The book is also carbon neutral. A forest in Norway was cut down to produce it but the good news is that another one was planted ... in England. The Norwegians have got too many anyway. You might like to know, ten per cent of every copy sold goes to a very worthwhile charity. Me. I have an over-draft and a hungry kid brother to support.

One last thing. Remember that this book comes with a MONEY BACK GUARANTEE. If for any reason you don't like it, Walker guarantee they won't give you back your money.

All the best,

Tim Diamond

The
FReNch
CoNFeCTioN

The French for Murder

Everybody loves Paris. There's an old guy who even wrote a song about it. "I love Paris in the springtime...", that's how it goes. Well, all I can say is, he obviously never went there with my big brother, Tim. I did – and it almost killed me.

It all started with a strawberry yoghurt.

It was a French strawberry yoghurt, of course, and it was all we had in the fridge for breakfast. Tim and I tossed a coin to decide who'd get the first mouthful. Then we tossed the coin to see who'd keep the coin. Tim won both times. So there I was sitting at the breakfast table chewing my nails, which was all I had to chew, when Tim suddenly let out a great gurgle and started waving his spoon in the air like he was trying to swat a fly.

"What is it, Tim?" I asked. "Don't tell me! You've found a strawberry!"

"No, Nick! Look...!"

He was holding up the silver foil that he'd just torn off the yoghurt carton and looking at it, and now I understood. The company that made the yoghurt was having one of those promotions. You've probably seen them on chocolate bars or crisps or Coke cans. These days you can't even open a can of beans without finding out if you've won a car or a holiday in Mexico or a cheque for a thousand pounds. Personally, I'm just grateful if I actually find some beans. Anyway, the yoghurt people were offering a whole range of prizes and there it was, written on the underside of the foil.

Congratulations from Bestlé Fruit Yoghurts! You have just won a weekend for two in Paris! Just telephone the number printed on the carton for further details and ... Bon Voyage!

"I've won, Nick!" Tim gasped. "A weekend for two...!" He stopped and bit his thumb. "Who shall I take?" he muttered.

"Oh thanks a lot, Tim," I said. "It was me who bought the yoghurt."

"But it was my money."

"If it hadn't been for me, you'd have spent it on a choc ice."

Tim scowled. "But Paris, Nick! It's the most romantic city in Europe. I want to take my girlfriend."

"Tim," I reminded him.

"You haven't got a girlfriend."

That was a bit cruel of me. The truth was, Tim hadn't been very lucky in love. His first serious relationship had ended tragically when his girlfriend had tried to murder him. After that he'd replied to one of those advertisements in the lonely hearts column of a newspaper, but he can't have read it properly because the girl had turned out to be a guy who spent the evening chasing him round Paddington station. His last girlfriend had been a fire eater in a local circus. He'd taken her out for a romantic, candlelit dinner but she'd completely spoiled it by eating the candles. Right now he was on his own. He sometimes said he felt like a monk – but without the haircut or the religion.

Anyway, we argued a bit more but finally he picked up the telephone and rang the number on the yoghurt carton. There was no answer.

"That's because you've telephoned the sell-by date," I told him. I turned the carton over. "This is the number here…"

And that was how, three weeks later, we found ourselves standing in the forecourt at the train station. Tim was carrying the tickets. I was carrying the bags. It had been more than a year since we'd been abroad – that had been to Amsterdam on the trail of the mysterious assassin known as Charon – and that time we had gone by ferry. Tim had been completely seasick even before he reached the sea. I was relieved that this time we were going by train, taking the Channel Tunnel, although with Tim, of course, you never knew.

We took the escalator down to the international terminal. Ahead of us, the tunnel was waiting: a thirty-two mile stretch linking England and France, built at a cost of twelve billion pounds.

"You have to admit," Tim said. "It's an engineering marvel."

"That's just what I was thinking," I said.

"Yes. It's a fantastic escalator. And so much faster than going down the stairs…"

We had two seats next to each other right in the middle of one of the carriages.

The train was pretty full and soon we were joined by two other passengers opposite us. They were both travelling alone. The first was from Texas – you could tell just from his hat. He was chewing an unlit cigar (this was a non-smoking compartment) and reading a magazine: *International Oil*. The other passenger was a very old lady with white hair and skin so wrinkled I was amazed it managed to stay on. I wasn't sure if she had huge eyes or extremely powerful spectacles but every time she looked at me I thought I was about to be hit by a pair of grey and white golf balls. I looked out of the window. The platform was already empty, sweeping in a graceful curve beneath the great glass canopy. Somewhere a door slammed.

The train left exactly on time at ten minutes past ten. There was no whistle. No announcement. I wouldn't have known we had moved if it hadn't been for the slight shudder – and even that was Tim, not the train. He was obviously excited.

About an hour later there was an announcement on the intercom and we dipped into the tunnel carved out underneath the sea. That was a non-event too. A car park, a sign advertising hamburgers, a white cement wall and suddenly the outside world disappeared to be replaced by rushing blackness. So this was the engineering miracle of the last century? As far as Eurostar was concerned, it was just a hole in the ground.

Tim had been ready with his camera and

now he drew back, disappointed. "Is this it?" he demanded.

I looked up from my book. "What were you expecting, Tim?" I asked.

"I thought this train went underwater!" Tim sighed. "I wanted to take some pictures of the fish!"

The other passengers had heard this and somehow it broke the silence. The old lady had been knitting what looked like a multi-coloured sack but now she looked up. "I love taking the train," she announced, and for the first time I realized that she was French. Her accent was so thick you could have wrapped yourself in it to keep warm.

"It sure is one hell of a thing," the Texan agreed. "London to Paris in three and a half hours. Great for business."

The Texan held up his magazine. "I'm in oil. Jed Mathis is the name."

"Why do you call your oil Jed Mathis?" Tim asked.

"I'm sorry?" Jed looked confused. He turned to the old lady. "Are you visiting your grandchildren in Paris?" he asked.

"Non!" the lady replied.

Tim dug into his pocket and pulled out a French dictionary. While he was looking up the word, she continued in English.

"I have a little cake shop in Paris. Erica Nice. That's my name. Please, you must try some of my almond slices." And before anyone could stop her, she'd pulled out a bag of cakes which she offered to us all.

We were still hurtling through the darkness. Tim put away his dictionary and

helped himself. At the same time, a steward approached us, pushing one of those trolleys piled up with sandwiches and coffee. He was a thin, pale man with a drooping moustache and slightly sunken eyes. The name on his badge was Marc Chabrol. I remember thinking even then that he looked nervous.

A nervous traveller, I thought. But then, why would a nervous traveller work on a train?

Jed produced a wallet full of dollars and offered to buy us all coffee. A free breakfast and we hadn't even arrived. Things were definitely looking up.

"So what do you do?" Erica Nice asked, turning to Tim.

Tim gave a crooked smile. It was meant to make him look smart but in fact he just looked as though he had toothache. "I'm a private detective," he said.

The steward dropped one of the coffee cups. Fortunately, he hadn't added the water yet. Coffee granules showered over the Kit-Kats.

"A private detective?" Erica trilled. "How very unusual!"

"Are you going to Paris on business?" the Texan asked.

Now of course the answer was "no". We were on holiday. Tim hadn't had any business for several weeks and even then he had only been hired to find a missing dog. In fact he had spent three days at Battersea Dogs' Home where he had been bitten three times – twice by dogs. The trouble was, though, he was never going to admit this. He liked to think of himself as a man of mystery. So now he winked and leaned forward. "Just between you and me," he drawled, "I'm on a case." Yes. A nutcase, I thought. But he went on. "I've been hired by Interplop."

"You mean Interpol," the Texan said.

"The International Police," Tim agreed. "It's a top-secret case. It's so secret, they don't even know about it at the top. In other words..." He gestured with his almond slice, spraying Jed with crumbs, "...a case for Tim Diamond."

The steward had obviously heard all this. As he put down the first cup of coffee, his hands were shaking so much that the liquid spilled over the table. His face had been pale to begin with. Now it had no colour at all. Even his moustache seemed to have faded.

"Where are you staying in Paris?" the old lady asked.

"It's a hotel called The Fat Greek," Tim said.

"Le Chat Gris," I corrected him. It was French for "grey cat" and this was the name of the hotel where Bestlé Yoghurts had booked us in for three nights.

The name seemed to have an electric effect on the steward. I'd been watching him out of the corner of my eye and actually saw him step backwards, colliding with the trolley. The bottles and cans shook. Two packets of gingerbread biscuits rocketed onto the floor. The man was terrified. But why?

"Paris is so beautiful in the spring," the old lady said. She'd obviously seen the effect that Tim was having on the steward and perhaps she was trying to change the subject before the poor man had a heart attack. "You must make sure you take a stroll on the Champs Elysées ... if you have the time."

"How much do I owe you for the coffee?" the American asked.

"Ten euros, monsieur..." The steward reached down and picked up the biscuits.

The way he took the money and moved off, he could have been trying to get to Paris ahead of the train. I guessed he wanted to get away from us as fast as he could. And I was right. He didn't even stop to offer anyone else in the carriage a coffee. He simply disappeared. Later, when I went to the loo, I saw the trolley standing on its own in the passageway.

Twenty minutes after we'd entered the tunnel, the train burst out again. There was nothing to show that we'd left one country and entered another. The French cows grazing in the fields looked just the same as the English ones on the other side. An official came past, looking at passports. Erica Nice looked at Tim as if puzzled in some way and went back to her knitting. Jed returned to his magazine. We didn't speak for the rest of the journey.

We arrived at the Gare du Nord about an hour later. As everyone struggled with their luggage, Tim gazed at the name. "When do we arrive in Paris?" he asked.

"Tim, this is Paris," I told him. "The Gare du Nord means north station. There are lots of stations in the city."

"I hope you have a lovely time," Erica Nice said. She had an old carpet-bag. It was big enough to hold a carpet – and maybe that was what she had been knitting. She winked at Tim. "Good luck with the case, mon ami!"

Meanwhile, the Texan had grabbed a leather briefcase. He nodded at us briefly and joined the queue for the exit. Tim and I retrieved our two bags and a few moments later we were standing on the platform, wondering which way to go.

"We'd better find the Metro," I said. Bestlé had given us some spending money for the weekend but I didn't think it would be enough for us to travel everywhere by taxi.

Tim shook his head. "Forget the Metro, Nick," he said. "Let's take the tube."

I didn't even bother to argue. I knew a little French – I'd been learning it from a little Frenchman who taught at our school – and I knew, for example, that Metro was the French word for tube train. On the other hand, I didn't know the French for idiot, which was the English word for Tim. I picked up the bags and prepared to follow him when suddenly we found ourselves interrupted.

It was Marc Chabrol. The French steward

had reappeared and was standing in front of us, blocking our way. He was terrified. I could see it in his bulging eyes, the sweat on his cheeks, the yellow and black bow tie which had climbed halfway up his neck.

"I have to talk to you, Monsieur," he rasped. He was speaking in English, the words as uncomfortable in his mouth as somebody else's false teeth. "Tonight. At eleven o'clock. There is a café in the sixth *arrondisement*. It is called La Palette..."

"That's very nice of you," Tim said. He seemed to think that Chabrol was inviting us out for a drink.

"Beware of the mad American!" The steward whispered the words as if he were too afraid to speak them aloud. "The mad American...!"

He was about to add something but then his face changed again. He seemed to freeze as if his worst nightmare had just come true. I glanced left and right but if there was someone he had recognized in the crowd, I didn't see them. *"Oh mon Dieu!"* he whispered. He seized Tim's hand and pressed something into the palm. Then he turned and staggered away.

Tim opened his hand. He was holding a small blue envelope with a gold star printed on the side. I recognized it at once. It was a sachet of sugar from the train. "What was all that about?" Tim asked.

I took the sugar and examined it. I thought he might have written something on it – a telephone number or something. But it was just a little bag of sugar. I slipped it into my back pocket. "I don't know..." I said. And I didn't. Why should the steward have left us with a spoonful of sugar? Why did he want to meet us later that night? What was going on?

"Funny people, the French," Tim said.

Ten minutes later, we were still at the Gare du Nord. The money that Bestlé had given us was in English pounds and pence. We needed euros and that meant queuing up at the Bureau de Change. The queue was a long one and it seemed to be moving at a rate of one euro per hour.

We had just reached the window when we heard the scream.

It was like no sound I had ever heard, thin and high and horribly final. The station was huge and noisy but the scream cut through the crowd like a scalpel. Everybody stopped and turned to see where it had come from. Even Tim heard it. "Oh dear," he said. "It sounds like someone has stepped on a cat."

Tim changed thirty pounds, and taking the money we moved in the direction of the Metro. Already a police car had arrived and several uniformed gendarmes were hurrying towards the trains. I strained to hear what the crowd was saying. They were speaking French, of course. That didn't make it any easier.

"What's happened?"

"It's terrible. Somebody has fallen under a train."

"It was a steward. He was on the train from London. He fell off a platform."

"Is he hurt?"

"He's dead. Crushed by a train."

I heard all of it. I understood some of it. I didn't like any of it. A steward? Off the London train? Somehow I didn't need to ask his name.

"Tim," I asked. "What's the French for murder?"

Tim shrugged. "Why do you want to know?"

"I don't know." I stepped onto the escalator and allowed it to carry me down. "I've just got a feeling it's something we're going to need."

Le Chat Gris

Le Chat Gris was in the Latin quarter, a dark, busy area on the south side of the River Seine. Here the streets were full of students and the smell of cheap food. It was a small, narrow building, wedged between an art gallery and a café. A metal cat, more rusty than grey, hung over the main entrance and there were brightly coloured flowers in the front windows. On closer inspection they turned out to be made of plastic.

The reception area was so small that if you went in too quickly you'd be out the other side. There was a receptionist standing behind the desk which was just as well as there wasn't enough room for a chair. He was an old man, at least sixty, with a crumpled face and something terribly wrong with his eyes. When he looked at our passports he had to hold them up beside his ear. He took our names, then sent us to a room on the fifth floor. Fortunately there was a lift but it wasn't much bigger than a telephone box. Tim and I stood shoulder to shoulder with our cases as it creaked and trembled slowly up. Next time, I decided, I'd take the stairs.

The truth was that Bestlé hadn't been too generous with the accommodation. Our room was built into the roof with wooden beams that sloped down at strange angles. It made me think of the Hunchback of Notre Dame. You needed a hunched back to avoid hitting your head on the ceiling. There were two beds, a single window with a view over the other rooftops, a chest of drawers and a bathroom too small to take a bath.

"Which bed do you want?" I asked.

"This one!" Tim threw himself onto the bed next to the window. There was a loud **PING** as several of the springs snapped. I sat down, more carefully, on the other bed. It felt like the duvet wasn't just filled with goose feathers, but they'd also left in half the goose.

We dumped our luggage and went out. This was, after all, Thursday morning and we only had until Sunday afternoon. Back in the reception area, the receptionist was talking to a new arrival. This was a square-shouldered man with narrow eyes and black, slicked-back hair. He was wearing an expensive, charcoal grey suit. Both of them stopped when they saw us. I dropped the key with a clunk.

"Merci," I said.

Neither of the men said anything. Maybe it was my accent.

There was a mirror next to the front door and but for that I wouldn't have noticed what happened next. But as Tim and I made our way out, the man in the grey suit reached out and took my key, turning it round so that he could read the number. He was interested in us. That was for sure. His eyes, empty of emotion, were still scrutinizing us as the door swung shut and we found ourselves in the street.

First the death of the steward on the train. Then the last whispered warning: *"Beware the mad American!"* And now this. There was a nasty smell in the air and already I knew it wasn't just French cheese.

"Which way, Nick?" Tim was waiting for me, holding a camera. He had already taken three photographs of the hotel, a streetlamp and a postbox and he was waiting for me in the morning sunlight. I wondered if he had remembered to put in a film.

I thought for a moment. I was probably being stupid. We were here in Paris for the weekend and nothing was going to happen. I couldn't even be sure that it really was Marc Chabrol who had fallen under the train. "Let's try down there," I said, pointing down the street.

"Good idea," Tim agreed as he turned the other way.

What can I tell you about Paris? I'm no travel writer. I'm not crazy about writing and I can't usually afford to travel. But anyway...

Paris is a big city full of French people. It's a lot prettier than London and for that matter so are the people. They're everywhere: in the street-side cafés, sipping black coffee from thimble-sized cups, strolling along the Seine in their designer sunglasses, snapping at each other on the bridges through eighteen inches of the latest Japanese lens. The streets are narrower than in London and looking at the traffic you get the feeling that war has broken out. There are cars parked everywhere. On the streets and on the pavements. Actually, it's hard to tell which cars are parked and which ones are just stuck in the traffic jams. But the strange thing is that nobody seems to be in a hurry. Life is just a big jumble that moves along at its own pace and if you're in a hurry to leave then maybe you should never have come there in the first place.

That first day, Tim and I did the usual tourist things. We went up the Eiffel Tower. Tim fainted. So we came down again. We went to the cathedral of Notre Dame and I took a picture of Tim and another of a gargoyle. I just hoped that when I got them developed I'd remember which was which. We went up the Champs Elysées and down the Jardin des Tuileries. By lunchtime, my stomach was rumbling. So, more worryingly, were my feet.

We had an early supper at a brasserie overlooking another brasserie. That's another thing about Paris. There are brasseries everywhere. Tim ordered two ham sandwiches, a beer for him and a Coke for me. Then I ordered them again using words the waiter understood. The sandwiches arrived: twenty centimetres of bread, I noticed, but only ten centimetres of ham.

"This is the life, eh, Nick?" Tim sighed as he sipped his beer.

"Yes, Tim," I said. "And this is the bill."

Tim glanced at it and swallowed his beer the wrong way. "Twenty euros!" he exclaimed. "That's ... that's...!" He frowned. "How much is that in pounds?"

"One euro is about seventy pence," I said.

"So that's..."

"Fourteen pounds," I did the maths for him. Otherwise we might be here all day.

"That's daylight robbery." Tim shook his head, "I hate foreign money."

"Only because you haven't got any," I said.

We were walking back in the direction of the hotel when it happened. We were in one of those quiet, antique streets near the Seine when two men appeared, blocking our way. The first was in his forties, tall and slim, wearing a white linen suit that was so crumpled and dirty, it hung off him like a used paper bag. He was one of the ugliest men I had ever seen. He had green eyes, a small nose and a mouth like a knife wound. None of these were in quite the right place. It was as if his whole face had been drawn by a six-year-old child.

His partner was about twenty years younger with the body of an ape and, if the dull glimmer in his eyes was anything to go by, a brain to match. He was wearing jeans and a leather jacket and smoking a cigarette. I guessed he was a body-builder. He had muscles bulging everywhere and a neck that somehow managed to be wider than his head. His hair was blonde and greasy. He had

fat lips and a tiny beard sprouting out of the middle of his chin.

"Good evening," White Suit said in perfect English. His voice came out like a whisper from a punctured balloon. "My name is Bastille. Jacques Bastille. My friend's name is Lavache. I wonder if I might speak with you."

"If you want to know the way, don't ask us!" Tim replied. "We're lost too."

"I'm not lost. Oh, no." Bastille smiled, revealing teeth the colour of French mustard. "No. But I want to know what he told you. I want to know what you know."

Tim turned to me, puzzled.

"What exactly do you mean?" I asked.

"The steward on the train. What did he tell you?" There was a pause. Then ... "Lavache!"

Bastille nodded and his partner produced

what looked like a little model of that famous statue, the Venus de Milo. You know the one. The naked woman with no arms that stands somewhere in the Louvre.

"No thank you," Tim began. "We're not..."

Lavache pressed a button and ten centimetres of razor-sharp metal sprang out of the head of the statue. It was a neat trick. I don't think the real statue ever did that.

Tim stared at it.

"Where is it?" Bastille demanded.

"Your friend's holding it in his hand!" Tim gasped.

"Not the knife! *Sacré bleu!* Are all the English such idiots? I am talking about the object. The item that you were given this morning at the Gare du Nord."

"I wasn't given anything!" Tim wailed.

"It's true," I said, even though I knew that it wasn't.

Bastille blinked heavily. "You're lying."

"No, we're not," Tim replied. "Cross my heart and hope to..."

"Tim!" I interrupted.

"KILL THEM BOTH!" Bastille snapped.

They really did mean to kill us there and then in that quiet Paris street. Lavache lifted the knife, his stubby fingers curving around the base, a bead of saliva glistening at the corner of his mouth. I glanced back, wondering if we could run. But it was hopeless. We'd be cut down before we could take a step.

"The older one first," Bastille commanded.

"That's him!" Tim said, pointing at me.

"Tim!" I exclaimed.

The knife hovered between us.

But then suddenly a party of American tourists turned the corner – about twenty of them, following a guide who was holding an umbrella with a Stars and Stripes attached to the tip. They were jabbering excitedly as they descended on us. There was nothing Bastille and Lavache could do. Suddenly they were surrounded, and realizing this was our only chance I grabbed hold of Tim and moved away, keeping a wall of American tourists between us and our attackers. Only when we'd come to the top of the street where it joined the wide and busy Boulevard St Michel did we break away and run.

But the two killers weren't going to let us get away quite so easily. I glanced back and saw them pushing their way through the crowd. Bastille shoved out a hand and one of the tourists, an elderly woman, shrieked and fell backwards into a fountain. Several of the other tourists stopped and took photographs of her. Bastille stepped into the road. A car swerved to avoid him and crashed into the front of a restaurant. Two lobsters and a plateful of mussels were sent flying. Someone screamed.

It still wasn't dark. The streets were full of people on their way to restaurants, too wrapped up in their own affairs to notice two English visitors running for their lives. I had no idea where I was going and I wasn't going to stop and ask for directions. I grabbed Tim again and steered him up an alleyway with dozens more restaurants on both sides.

 A waiter in a long white apron, carrying several trays laden

with plates and glasses, stepped out in front of me. There was no way I could avoid him. There was a strangled cry, then a crash.

"Excusez-moi!" Tim burbled.

Fortunately, I didn't know enough French to understand the waiter's reply.

The alleyway brought us back to the Seine. I could see Notre Dame in the distance. Only a few hours before we had been standing on one of its towers, enjoying the view. How could our holiday have become a nightmare so quickly?

"THIS WAY, TIM!" I shouted.

I pulled him across a busy street, cars screeching to a halt, horns blaring. A gendarme turned round to face us, a whistle clenched between his teeth, his hands scrabbling for his gun. I swear he would have shot us except that we were already on the other side of the road and a few seconds later Bastille had reached him, brutally pushing him out of the way. The unfortunate gendarme spun round and collided with a cyclist. Both of them collapsed in a tangle of rubber and steel. The last I saw of the gendarme, he had got back to his feet and was shouting at us, making a curious, high-pitched noise. Evidently he had swallowed his whistle which had now got lodged in his throat.

The river was now right in front of us with a pedestrian bridge leading over to the other side. Bastille and Lavache were already crossing the road, blocked for a moment by a bus that had slipped in between them and us.

"The river!" I said.

Tim reached into his pocket and took out his camera.

"NO!" I yelled. **"I DON'T WANT YOU TO PHOTOGRAPH IT! I WANT US TO CROSS IT!"**

We ran onto the bridge, but I hadn't taken more than a few steps before I saw that we'd made a bad mistake. The bridge was closed. There was a tall barrier running across the middle of it with a MEN AT WORK sign – but no sign at all of any men actually at work. They had left their tools, though. There was a wheelbarrow, a pile of steel girders, a cement mixer ... even if we could have climbed over the fence it would have been hard to get through.

"WE'VE GOT TO GO BACK!" I shouted.

But it was too late. Bastille and Lavache

had already arrived at the entrance to the bridge and were moving more slowly, both of them smiling. They knew they had us trapped. Lavache had his knife out. It was difficult to hear with the noise of the traffic, but I think he was humming.

We couldn't go back. We couldn't climb the fence. If we jumped over the side, we'd probably drown. This was only March and the water would be ice-cold. Just twenty metres separated us from the two Frenchmen. There was nothing we could do.

And that was when I saw the boat. It was what they called a *Bateau Mouche*, one of those long, elegant boats with glass windows and ceilings that carry tourists up and down the river throughout the day and night. This one was full of people enjoying a dinner and dance. I heard the music drifting up to us. They were playing a waltz, the "Blue Danube". A strange choice considering they were on the Seine. Already the boat was slipping under the bridge. Another few seconds and it would have disappeared down towards the Eiffel Tower.

"JUMP, TIM!" I ordered.

"Right, Nick!" Tim jumped up and down on the spot.

"No. I mean – jump off the bridge!"

"What?" Tim looked at me as if I was mad.

Bastille was only five steps away from us now. I ran to the edge of the bridge, hoisted myself up and jumped. Tim did the same, a few seconds behind me. I caught a glimpse of Bastille, staring at us, his face twisted between anger and amazement. Then I was falling through space with the river, the bridge and the boat corkscrewing around me. I thought I might have mistimed it but then my feet hit something and I crashed onto the deck. I was lucky. I had hit the front of the boat where there was a sheet of tarpaulin stretched out amid a tangle of ropes. It broke my fall.

Tim was less fortunate. He had jumped a few seconds after me, allowing the boat to travel a few metres further forward. I heard the glass shatter as he went feet first through the glass roof. There were more screams and the music stopped. I pulled myself up and gazed groggily through a window. Tim had landed on one of the tables and was lying there, sprawled out, surrounded by broken plates and glasses and with what looked like a whole roast duck in his lap.

"Que fais-tu? Qu'est-ce que se passe?"

A man in a blue uniform had appeared on the deck. He was staring at me in horror. It was the captain of the Bateau Mouche. There were a couple of waiters with him. I didn't even struggle as the three of them grabbed hold of me. I wondered if they were going to lock me up or throw me over the side. Certainly it didn't look as if they were going to invite me in for a dance and something to eat.

I twisted round and took one last look back at the bridge. Bastille and Lavache were leaning over the side, watching, and as I was dragged inside they vanished, swallowed up in the gathering gloom.

Down and Out

You won't meet many thirteen-year-olds who have been locked up in prisons on both sides of the Channel, but I'm one of them. I did time in Strangeday Hall, sharing a cell with Johnny Powers, England's public enemy number one*, and here I was in prison in Paris, this time with Tim. It was half past nine in the evening. We'd been given dinner – bread and water – but the fact that it was French bread and Perrier didn't make it taste any better.

* See Public Enemy Number Two

Miraculously, neither Tim nor I had been hurt jumping from the bridge. The captain had locked us both up in the kitchen on board the ship and by the time we docked, the police were already waiting. I suppose he must have radioed on ahead. I hadn't tried to argue as we were thrown into the back of a van and driven at high speed through the streets of Paris. Nobody spoke English and even if they had they wouldn't have believed us. I assumed they'd call the British consul or someone. I would leave the explanations until then.

Neither of us had said anything for a while but at last Tim broke the silence. "That's the last time I buy a Bestlé yoghurt," he muttered.

"It wasn't their fault, Tim," I said, although I knew how he felt. We hadn't even been in

Paris one day and we'd witnessed one murder, been chased by two killers and were now locked up ourselves. It was probably just as well that we weren't planning to stay a whole week. "I just wish I knew what it was all about," I added.

"They tried to kill us, Nick," Tim explained. "They nearly *did* kill us!"

"I noticed, Tim. But why?"

Tim thought for a moment. "Perhaps they don't like foreigners?" he suggested.

"No. They were looking for something. Something they thought we had." I already knew it had to be tied in with Marc Chabrol, the steward we had met at the Gare du Nord, and the sachet of sugar he had given us. But what could be so important about a packet of sugar? It was still in my back pocket. I reached in and took it out. "This is what they were after," I said.

"Sugar?"

"Unless there's something else inside..."

I was about to open it there and then but at that moment the door opened and a young policeman with close-cropped hair and glasses walked in. I slipped the sachet back into my pocket. I could always examine it later.

"This way, please," the policeman said.

He led us back out and down a corridor, then into an interrogation room that smelled of cigarette smoke. There was a table and three chairs but nothing else, not even a window. A naked light bulb hung on a short flex from the ceiling. The policeman gestured and we all sat down.

"You are English," he said.

"That's right," I said. The man obviously had a first-class brain.

"This is an outrage!" Tim exclaimed. "You can't keep us here. I demand to speak to the British ambassador! If the British ambassador is busy, I'll speak to his wife."

The policeman leaned forward. "First of all, monsieur, I can keep you here for as long as I wish," he said. "And secondly, I doubt very much that the British ambassador would be interested in you. Or his wife!"

"Why wouldn't he be interested in his wife?" Tim asked.

The policeman ignored him. "You and your small brother have caused great damage to one of our Bateaux Mouches," he went on. "It is most fortunate that nobody was injured.

I wish to know why the two of you jumped off the bridge. You were trying to commit suicide, perhaps? Or could it have been a joke?"

"It was no joke," I said. "There were two men trying to kill us..."

The policeman looked at me in disbelief.

"It's true," I went on. "They said their names were Bastille and Lavache. They had a knife..."

"Tell me your names," the policeman commanded. He took out a notebook and prepared to write.

"I'm Tim Diamond," Tim said. "You may have heard of me."

"No, monsieur..."

"Well, I'm a well-known detective back in London." Tim pointed at the notebook. "That's the capital of England," he added, helpfully.

The policeman paused and took a deep breath. He was getting older by the minute. "I am aware of that," he said. "May I ask, what is your business here in Paris?"

"Of course you can ask!" Tim said.

The policeman groaned. "What is your business?" he demanded.

"We're on holiday," I told him. "We only arrived today. We're staying in Le Chat Gris in the Latin quarter..."

The policeman looked at me strangely, as if he were seeing me properly for the first time. "Le Chat Gris..." he repeated. He closed the notebook. "Could you please wait here for a minute."

He stood up and left the room.

In fact it was ten minutes before he returned. The moment he walked in, I noticed there was something different about him. He was brisk, emotionless. And when he spoke, he did his best not to meet our eyes. "I have spoken with my superior officer," he said. "And he says that you are free to go!"

"How can we be free to go when we're locked up in here?" Tim asked.

"No, no, no, monsieur. He says that you may leave."

"They're unlocking the door and letting us out," I explained.

"As far as we are concerned, this incident is closed." The policeman did the same to his notebook.

"What about Bastille and Lavache?" I asked.

"We have no record of these men. It is our view that they do not exist!"

"What?"

"You jump off the bridge for a joke or maybe as a game and you make up the story of the killers to explain your actions. That is the view of my Superintendent."

"Well, he can't be as super as all that," I growled.

But there was no point arguing. For whatever their reasons, the French police had decided to let us go. As far as I was concerned, I just wanted to get out of jail. And out of Paris too, for that matter. I'd only been there for a day but so far our visit had been less fun than a French lesson – and twice as dangerous.

"Let's go, Tim," I said.

And we went.

It was almost eleven o'clock by the time we got back to the Latin quarter, but the night wasn't over yet. Tim wanted to stop for a beer and I was still anxious to open the packet of sugar that was burning a hole in my back pocket. We looked for a café and quite by coincidence found ourselves outside an old-fashioned, artistic sort of place whose name I knew. It was La Palette, the very same café where the train steward, Marc Chabrol, had asked us to meet.

He wasn't there, of course. Right now, if Chabrol was sipping coffee, it was with two wings and a halo. But there was someone there that we recognized. He was sitting out in the front, smoking a cigar, gazing into the night sky. There was no way I'd forget the hat. It was Jed Mathis, the businessman we had met on the train.

Tim saw him. "It's Ned," he said.

"You mean Jed," I said.

"Why don't we join him?"

"Forget it!" I grabbed Tim and we walked forward, continuing towards our hotel.

"But Nick! He paid for the drinks on the train. Maybe he'd buy me a beer."

"Yes, Tim. But think for a minute. What's he doing at La Palette?" I looked at my watch. It was eleven o'clock exactly. "It could just be a coincidence. But maybe he's waiting for someone. Maybe he's waiting for us! Don't you remember what Marc Chabrol said?"

"He asked us if we wanted to buy a KitKat."

"Yes. But after that. In the station, he warned us about someone who he called 'the mad American'. Jed Mathis is American! He said he was from Texas."

"You think Mathis killed Chabrol?"

"Mathis was on the train. And Chabrol ended up underneath it. I don't know. But I don't think we should hang around and have drinks with him. I think we should go home!"

We hurried on. Le Chat Gris loomed up ahead of us, but before we got there I noticed something else.

There was a man standing opposite the hotel. It was hard to recognize him because he was holding a camera up to his face, taking a picture. I heard the click of the button and the whir as the film wound on automatically. He wasn't a tourist. That much was certain. Not unless his idea of a holiday snap was two English tourists about to check out. Because the photograph he had taken had been of us. There could be no doubt about it. I could feel the telephoto lens halfway up my nose.

He lowered the camera and now I recognized the man. He had been standing in the reception area that morning when we left: a dark-haired man in a grey suit.

Marc Chabrol, the steward.

Bastille and Lavache.

And now this.

Just what was happening in Paris and why did it all have to happen to us?

A car suddenly drew up, a blue Citroën. The man with the camera got in and a moment later they were roaring past us. I just caught a glimpse of the driver, smoking a cigarette with one hand, steering with the other. Then they were gone.

Tim had already walked into the hotel. Feeling increasingly uneasy, I followed him in.

We took the key from the squinting receptionist and took the stairs back to the top
of the hotel. There were a lot of them and
the stairway was so narrow that the walls
brushed both my shoulders as I climbed.
Finally we got to the last floor. Tim stopped
for breath. Then he unlocked our door.

Our room had been torn apart. The sheets
had been pulled off the bed and the mat-
tress slashed open, springs and enough hair
to cover a horse tumbling out onto the floor.
Every drawer had been opened, upturned
and smashed. The carpet had been pulled
up and the curtains down. Tim's jackets
and trousers had been scattered all over the
room. And I mean scattered. We found one
arm on a window-sill, one leg in the shower, a
single pocket under what was left of the bed.

Our suitcases had been cut open and turned inside out. We'd need another suitcase just to carry the old ones down to the bin.

Tim gazed at the destruction. "I can't say I think too much of room service, Nick," he said.

"THIS ISN'T ROOM SERVICE, TIM!" I exploded. **"THE ROOM'S BEEN SEARCHED!"**

"What do you think they were looking for?"

"This!" I took out the packet of sugar. Once again I was tempted to open it – but this wasn't the right time. "This is the only thing Chabrol gave us back at the station. It must be the object that Bastille was talking about." I slid it back into my pocket, then thought again. It seemed that Bastille was

determined to get his hands on the sugar.
I wouldn't be safe carrying it. It was better
to leave it in the hotel room. After all, they'd
already searched the place once. It was
unlikely they'd think of coming back.

I looked around, then slid the sugar into the toilet roll in the bathroom, inside the cardboard tube. Nobody would notice it there and the police could pick it up later. Because that was the next step.

"We've got to call the police," I said.

"We've just come from the police," Tim reminded me.

"I know. But if they see our room, they've got to believe us. And as soon as they're here, I'll show them the packet. Maybe they'll be able to work the whole thing out."

I looked for the telephone and eventually found it – or what was left of it. You'd have to be an expert at electronics or at least very good at jigsaws to use it again.

"Why don't we talk to the man downstairs?" Tim asked.

I thought of the squinting receptionist. Only that morning he'd been talking to the man in the grey suit, the one who'd just taken our photograph.

"I don't trust him," I said. At that moment I wouldn't have trusted my own mother.

Tim held up a short-sleeved shirt. It had been a long-sleeved shirt when he had packed it. He looked as if he was going to burst into tears. At least he could use the rest of the shirt as a handkerchief if he did.

"Let's go back down, Tim," I said. "We can call the police from the lobby. I noticed a phone booth."

"What's the French for 999?" Tim asked.

"17," I replied. I'd seen it written next to the phone.

But the phone in the hotel was out of order.

There was a sign on the window reading *"Hors de service"*. I translated for Tim and he went over to the receptionist. "We want to call the police," he said.

"Please?" The receptionist narrowed his eye. I think he would have liked to have narrowed both his eyes, but the one on the left wasn't working.

"No," Tim explained. "Police." He saluted and bent his knees, doing an imitation of a policeman. The receptionist stared at him as if he had gone mad.

"Les flics," I said.

"Ah!" The receptionist nodded. Then he leant forward and pointed. "You go out the door. You turn left. Then you take the first turning left again," he growled. He actually spoke pretty good English even if the words had trouble getting past his throat. "There's a police station just at the next corner."

We left the hotel, turned left and then immediately left again. We found ourselves in a narrow alleyway that twisted its way through the shadows before coming to a brick wall.

"This is wrong," I said.

"You don't want to go to the police anymore?" Tim asked.

"No, Tim. I still want to go to the police but this is the wrong way. It's a dead-end."

"Maybe we have to climb over the wall."

"I don't think so..."

I was getting worried. After everything that had happened to us so far, the last place I wanted to be was a dead-end ... or anywhere else with the word "dead" in it.

And I was right. There was a sudden squeal as a van appeared racing towards us. The squeal, incidentally, came from Tim. The van was reversing. For a moment I thought it was going to crush us, but it stopped, just centimetres away. The back doors flew open. Two men got out.

Everything was happening too quickly. I couldn't even tell who the men were or if I had seen them before. I saw one of them lash out and Tim spun round, crumpling to the ground. Then it was my turn. Something hard hit me on the back of the head. My legs buckled. I fell forward and one of the men must have caught me as I felt myself being half-pushed, half-carried into the back of the van.

Tim was next to me. "Some holiday!" he said.

Then either they hit me again or they hit him. Or maybe they hit both of us. Either way, I was out cold.

Paris by Night

I knew I was in trouble before I even opened my eyes. For a start, I was sitting up. If everything that had happened up until now had been a horrible dream – which it should have been – I would be lying in my nice warm bed in Camden with the kettle whistling in the kitchen and maybe Tim doing the same in the bath. But not only was I sitting in a hard, wooden chair, my feet were tied together with something that felt suspiciously like parcel tape and my hands were similarly bound behind my back. When I did finally open my eyes, it only got worse. Tim was next to me looking pale and confused ... by which I mean even more confused than usual. And Bastille and Lavache were sitting opposite us, both of them smoking.

The four of us were in a large, empty room that might once have been the dining room of a grand château but was now empty and dilapidated. The floor was wooden and the walls white plaster, with no pictures or deco-rations. A broken chandelier hung from the ceiling. In fact quite a lot of the ceiling was hanging from the ceiling. Half of it seemed to be peeling off.

I had no idea how much time had passed

since they'd knocked us out and bundled us into the back of a delivery van. An hour? A week? I couldn't see my watch – it was pinned somewhere behind me, along with the wrist it was on – so I twisted round and looked out of the window. The glass was so dust-covered that I could barely see outside, but from the light I would have said it was early evening. If so, we had been unconscious for about fifteen hours! I wondered where we were. Somewhere in the distance I thought I heard singing, the sound of a choir. But the music was foreign – and not French. It sounded vaguely religious, which made me think of churches. And that made me think of funerals. I just hoped they weren't singing for us.

"Good evening," Bastille muttered. He hadn't changed out of the dirty linen suit he had been wearing when we met him the day before. It was so crumpled now that I wondered if he had slept in it.

"What time is it?" Tim asked.

"It is time for you to talk!" Bastille blew a cloud of smoke into Tim's face.

Tim coughed. "You know those things can damage your health!" he remarked.

Not quickly enough, I thought. But I said nothing.

"It is *your* health that should concern you, my friend," Bastille replied.

"I'm perfectly well, thank you," Tim said.

"I mean – your health if you fail to tell us what we want to know!" Bastille's green eyes flared. He was even uglier when he was angry. "You have put us to a great deal of trouble," he went on. "We've searched you and this morning we searched your room. Are you going to tell us where it is?"

"It's on the top floor of the hotel!" Tim exclaimed.

"Not the room!" Bastille swore and choked on his cigarette. "I am talking about the packet that you were given by Marc Chabrol."

"The ex-steward," Lavache added. He giggled, and, looking at his ape-like hands, I suddenly knew how Chabrol had managed to "fall" under a train.

I'd said nothing throughout all this. I was just glad that I'd decided not to bring the packet with us. The two men must have searched Tim and me while we were unconscious. They had found nothing and it looked like they weren't going to go back and search the hotel room a second time.

"He gave us a cup of coffee," Tim was saying. "But we drank it. Unless you're talking about ... wait a minute..."

"Who *are* you people?" I cut in. I didn't want him to say any more. So long as we had the sachet, they wouldn't kill us. They needed to know where it was. But the moment they heard it was hidden in the toilet, we were dead. That much was certain. I would just have to keep them talking and hope for the best. "Look..." I went on. "The steward didn't give us anything. We're just here on holiday."

"*Non, non, non!*" Bastille shook his head. "Do not try lying to me, *mon petit ami*. I know that your brother is a private detective. I also know that he was sent to Paris by Interpol. I know that he is working on a special assigment." His face turned ugly, which, with his face, wasn't difficult. "Now I want you to tell me how much you know and who gave you your information."

"But I don't know anything!" Tim wailed.

He'd never spoken a truer word in his life. Tim knew nothing about any special assignment. He'd have had trouble telling anyone his own shoe size. And he also hadn't realized that this was all his fault. If only he'd kept his mouth shut on the train! He'd told Jed Mathis and the old woman that he was working for Interpol. Could one of them have passed it on? Jed Mathis...?

Beware the mad American...

It was too late to worry about that. I realized that Tim was still talking. He had told them everything. The competition on the yoghurt pot. The free weekend. The truth.

"He's right," I admitted. "We're just tourists. We're not working for anyone."

"It was a strawberry yoghurt!" Tim burbled. "Bestlé yoghurts. They're only eighty calories each..."

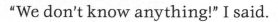

"We don't know anything!" I said.

Bastille and Lavache moved closer to each other and began to mutter in low, dark voices. I couldn't understand a word they were saying, but somehow I didn't like the sound of it. I tried to break free from the chair but it was useless. Things weren't looking good. By now they must have realized that they were wrong about us, that we were exactly what we said. But they weren't just going to order us a taxi and pretend the whole thing had never happened. As they're always saying in the old movies ... we knew too much. I still had no idea who they were or what they were doing, but we knew their names and had seen their faces. That was enough.

The two men straightened up. "We have decided that we believe you," Bastille said.

"That's terrific!" Tim exclaimed.

"So now we are going to kill you."

"Oh!" His face fell.

Lavache walked to the far side of the room and I strained my neck to watch him. He reached out with both hands and suddenly a whole section of the wall slid to one side. I realized now that it wasn't a wall at all but a set of floor-to-ceiling doors. There was another room on the other side, filled with activity, and at that moment I realized what this was all about. Perhaps I should have guessed from the start.

Drugs.

The other room was a laboratory. I could see metal tables piled high with white powder. More white powder being weighed on complicated electronic scales. White powder being spooned into plastic bags. There were about half-a-dozen people working there, young men and women with dirty faces but pristine laboratory coats. They were handling the white powder in complete silence, as if they knew that it was death they were carrying in their hands and that if it heard them it would somehow find them out.

Lavache lumbered into the room, vanishing from sight. When he reappeared, he was holding something which he handed to Bastille. Right then I was more scared than I've ever been in my life, and you know me ... I don't scare easily. But suddenly I remembered that I was thirteen years old, that I hadn't started shaving yet and that my mother (who'd been shaving for years) was thousands of miles away. I was so scared I almost wanted to cry.

Bastille was holding a bottle of pills.

He approached Tim first. "These are super-strength," he said. "I think five of them will be enough."

"No, thank you," Tim said. "I haven't got a headache."

"They're not headache pills, Tim," I said.

Bastille grabbed hold of Tim and forced his mouth open. He had counted five pills into the palm of his hand and I watched, powerless, as he forced them down Tim's throat. Then he turned and began to walk towards me.

"They don't taste very nice!" I heard Tim say, but then I'd gone crazy, rocking back and forth, yelling, kicking with my feet, trying to tear apart the parcel tape around my wrists. It was useless. I felt Lavache grab hold of my shoulders while at the same time, Bastille took hold of my chin. I don't know what was worse. Feeling his bony fingers against my face or knowing there was nothing I could do as he forced my mouth open. His right hand came up and the next moment there were four or five pills on my tongue. They had an evil taste. I drew a breath, meaning to spit them out, but his hand was already over my mouth, almost suffocating me. I screamed silently and felt the pills trickle down the back of my throat. I almost felt them drop into the pit of my stomach. Then Bastille pulled his hand clear and my head sank forward. I said nothing. I thought I was dead. I thought he had killed me.

Things happened very quickly after that. It seemed to me that the lights in the room had brightened and that somebody had turned up the heating. My eyes were hurting. And then the walls began to revolve, slowly at first, like the start of a ride at a funfair. But there was nothing fun about this. Drugs are poison and I was sure I had just been given a lethal overdose. I was sweating. I tried to speak but my tongue refused to move; anyway, my mouth was too dry.

I heard the parcel tape being ripped off and felt my hands come free. Lavache was standing behind me. I tried to look at him, but my head lolled uselessly. He pulled me off the chair and carried me outside. Bastille followed with Tim.

There was a white van waiting for us in an enclosed courtyard – we could have been anywhere. I looked back at the house we had just left. It was a grey building, three storeys high.

Most of its paint had flaked off and there were scorch marks, as if it had been involved in a fire. About half the windows were shattered. Others had been bricked in. The place looked derelict. I guessed it was supposed to.

I was bundled into the van and the next moment the engine started up, roaring at me like a mechanical beast. I almost expected it to come bursting through the floor, to gobble me up. The noise hammered at my ears and I groaned. Tim was thrown in next to me. The doors slammed. My stomach heaved. We were off.

There was a small window set in the door and I managed to stagger over to it and pull myself onto my knees to look out. But it was hard to see anything. The world was spinning faster now, tilting from side to side. I just made out a series of letters in red neon, but it seemed to take me for ever to work out the three words they formed:

THE FRENCH CONFECTION

The van turned a corner and I lost my balance. Before I fell, I caught a glimpse of a blue star ... on a flag or perhaps on the side of a building. Then the sound of the van's engine rose up again and swallowed me. The floor hit me in the face. Or maybe it was me who had hit the floor. I no longer knew the difference.

The journey took an hour ... a month ... a year. I no longer had any idea. What was the stuff they had given me? Whatever it was, it was taking over, killing me. I could feel it happening, an inch at a time. The van stopped. Hands that no longer belonged to bodies pulled us out. Then the pavement slapped me in the face, there was another scream from the engine and suddenly I knew that we were alone.

"Tim...?" I gasped the word. But Tim was no longer there. He had turned into some horrible animal with sixteen eyes, tentacles and...

I forced myself to concentrate, knowing that it was the drug that was doing it to me. The image dissolved and there he was again. My brother.

"Nick..." He staggered to his feet. All three of them. Things weren't back to normal yet.

The sky changed from red to blue to yellow to green. I stood up as well.

"Must get help," I said.

Tim groaned.

We were back in the centre of Paris. It was late at night. And Paris had never looked like this before.

There was the Seine but the water had gone, replaced by red wine that glowed darkly in the moonlight. It was twisting its way underneath the bridges, but now that I looked more closely, I saw that they had changed too. They had become huge sticks of French bread. There was a sudden buzzing. A Bateau Mouche had suddenly sprouted huge blue wings and legs. It leapt out of the water and onto one of the bridges, tearing a great chunk out with a hideous, hairy mouth before spiralling away into the night.

The ground underneath my feet had gone soft and I realized I was sinking into it. With a cry I lifted one foot and saw that the tar had melted and was dripping off my trainer. Except the tar was yellow, not black.

"It's cheese!" I shouted. And it was. The entire street had turned into cheese - soft, ripe, French cheese. I gasped for air, choking on the smell. At the same time, the cheese pulled me into it. Another few seconds and I would be sucked underneath the surface.

"Nick!" Tim called out.

And then the cheese was gone as he pointed with an arm that was now a mile long. There was a snail coming down the Boulevard. No ... not one snail but a thousand of them, each one the size of a house, slithering along ahead of the traffic, leaving a grey, slimy trail behind them. At one corner, the traffic lights had gone red and all the snails were squeaking at each other, a fantastic traffic jam of snails.

At the same time, I heard what sounded like a gigantic burp and a frog, the size of a bus, bounded across my vision, leaping over a building. But the frog was missing its legs. It was supporting itself on giant crutches.

The world twisted, heaved, broke up and then reformed with all the pieces in different positions: a jigsaw in the hands of a destructive child.

Suddenly we were surrounded by grinning stone figures, jabbering and staring at us with empty stone eyes. I recognized them: the gargoyles from Notre Dame. There must have been a hundred of them. One of them was sitting on Tim's shoulder like a grey chimpanzee. But Tim didn't seem to have noticed it.

Light. Car lights. Everywhere. A horn sounded. I had stepped into the road – but it didn't matter because the cars were the size of matchboxes. They were all Citroëns. Every one of them. And they were being followed by cyclists. The Tour de France had come early that year. All the cyclists were smoking cigarettes.

Tim was clutching a streetlamp. Now he was wearing a striped jersey and a beret and there was a string of onions hanging from his side. *"Je suis,"* he said. *"Tu es, il est..."*

I opened my mouth to reply.

CRASH! CRASH! CRASH!

I saw it before he did. Perhaps he didn't see it at all. Even now, with the drug pumping through my body, I knew that it wasn't real, that I was hallucinating. But it made no difference. As far as I was concerned, everything I saw was real. And if it was real, it could kill me. It could step on me. It could crush me.

The Eiffel Tower! On our first day in Paris we had crossed the city to visit it. Now the Eiffel Tower was coming to visit us. There it was, walking across Paris, swinging one iron foot, then the next, moving like some sort of giant, four-legged crab. One of its feet came down in a pancake stall. Wood shattered. Pancakes flew in all directions. Somebody screamed.

The cheese was getting softer. I was sinking into a boulevard of Brie, a dual carriageway of Camembert. The squirming yellow slipped round my waist, rose over my shoulder and twisted round my neck. I didn't even try to fight. I'd had enough. I waited for it to pull me under.

I thought I was going to die and if I'd waited another minute I might well have. But just then I heard what I thought was an owl, hooting in my ear. At the same time, I found myself staring at a face I knew. A dark-haired man in a grey-coloured suit. I became aware of a blue flashing light which either belonged to a dragon or a police car. I looked up and saw something driving out of the moon, flying through the sky towards me. An ambulance.

"Don't go to sleep!" a voice commanded. "Don't go to sleep! Don't go to sleep!"

But it was too late. I went to sleep.

For ever.

The Mad American

"You're lucky to be alive," the man said.

It was two days later. I don't want to tell you about those two days. I'd spent both of them in hospital in Paris and all I can say is, if you've ever had your stomach pumped, you'll know there are plenty of things you can do that are more fun. I don't remember much about the first day. The next day, I felt like a spin-drier that's been left on too long. All I'd eaten in the entire time was a little bread and water. Fortunately, the water didn't have bubbles. I don't think I could have managed the bubbles.

And now, here I was in the headquarters of Sûreté, the French police force. It's funny how police stations are the same the whole world over. This may have been grander and smarter than New Scotland Yard. The curtains were velvet and the pictures on the wall showed some grey-haired Frenchman in a suit rather than our own grey-haired Queen in a crown. But it still smelled the same.

Tim was sitting next to me. He was the colour of the yoghurt that had brought us here in the first place, with eyes like crushed strawberries. His hair was dishevelled and he looked like he hadn't slept in a month. I was going to say something but decided against it. I probably looked just as bad.

We were in the office of the Chief of Police – a man called Christien Moire. I knew because I'd seen the name and title on the door. It was on his desk too. Maybe he was worried he was going to forget it. He was the man in the grey suit whom I'd seen standing outside Le Chat Gris, the man who had been talking to the receptionist and who had later taken our photograph. Things were beginning to add up even if I still had no idea of the sum total.

"Another one hour and it would have been too late," Moire went on. He spoke English as if he had no idea what he was saying, lingering on every word. He had the sort of accent you get in bad television plays: *Anuzzer wan our an' eet would 'ave bin too late*. I hope you get the idea. "You were very lucky," he added.

"Sure," I muttered. "And we'd have been even luckier if you'd arrived a couple of hours before."

Moire shrugged. "I'm sorry," he said. But his dark, empty eyes looked about as apologetic as two lumps of ice. "We had no idea you had been taken," he went on.

"Who are you?" Tim demanded. "You call yourself the Sûreté. But what exactly are you sure about?"

"The Sûreté," Moire repeated, "is the French police force. I am the head of a special unit fighting the traffic in…"

"…drugs." I completed the sentence.

"*Exactement.* I have to say that you and your brother seem to have turned up in the wrong place at the wrong time. If I hadn't been watching you..."

"You were at the hotel," I said. "I saw you outside. You had a camera..."

"Is that your hobby?" Tim asked. "Photography?"

Christien Moire stared at Tim through narrow eyes. He obviously hadn't ever met anyone like him before. "Le Chat Gris has been under surveillance," he said. "Perhaps I should explain..."

"Perhaps you should," I said.

Moire lit a Gauloise. It's a funny thing about the French. Not only do they all smoke, but they smoke the most horrible cigarettes in the world. Forget about the health warning on the packet. The smoke from Moire's cigarette was so thick, you could have printed it on that.

"For some time now," he began, "we have been aware of a drug-smuggling operation. Somebody has been moving drugs to London ... using the trains under the channel. We still don't know how they're doing it. We have searched the trains from top to bottom but we have found nothing. Worse still, we do not know who they are."

"Is there anything you *do* know?" I asked.

Moire glanced at me with unfriendly eyes. "We know only the code-name of the man behind the operation," he replied.

"The Mad American," I said.

That surprised Moire, but he tried not to show it. "The drugs arrive from Marseilles," he went on. "They are weighed and packaged somewhere in Paris. Then the Mad American arranges for them to be sent to London.

We've been working with the English police to try to stop them. So far we have had no success in London. But in Paris we had one lucky break."

"Le Chat Gris," I said.

"Yes, we learned that the hotel is sometimes used by the Mad American. When dealers arrive from London to buy his drugs, that is where they stay. He meets them there. They pay him the money and then his two associates – Jacques Bastille and Luc Lavache – arrange for the drugs to be sent on the train."

"So *that's* why you photographed us!" I said. "You thought we'd come to Paris to buy drugs!"

"I know it sounds unlikely," Moire said. "An English kid and his idiotic brother –"

"Nick isn't idiotic!" Tim protested.

"We became interested in you the moment you reported that Bastille and Lavache had attempted to kill you," Moire went on. "I ordered the photograph to be taken so that we could check you against our criminal files."

"But if you thought we were criminals, why did you let us go in the first place?" I asked. It had puzzled me at the time, the policeman suddenly changing his mind and telling us we could leave.

"The answer to that is simple," Moire said. "We still had no idea what part you had to play in all this, but you had mentioned Le Chat Gris and that was enough. It was important that the Mad American should not be aware that the police were involved. I personally ordered your release, and at the same time I made sure that we kept you under – how do you say? – surveillance. This was very lucky for you, considering how things turned out."

"You were following us."

"Yes. I saw you go back to the hotel, and minutes later I saw the van with the two men who knocked you out and kidnapped you. We followed the van but unfortunately lost it in traffic..."

"...so you don't know where we were taken."

"No. But I knew that you were in danger and I had every gendarme in Paris looking out for you. One of them saw you and radioed HQ. By that time they had pumped you with enough drugs to kill a horse."

"Why would they want to kill a horse?" Tim asked.

Moire ignored him. "We only got to you in the nick of time. Another ten minutes, and

the two of you would now be in Père Lachaise."

"You mean, another hotel," Tim said.

"No. Père Lachaise is a cemetery."

"OK. You saved us, Monsieur Moire," I said. "But now, if you don't mind, I'm heading back to the hotel, packing and leaving for London."

"That's right, Monsieur Loire," Tim agreed. "We're out of here!"

"I'm afraid not." Moire hadn't raised his voice. If anything, he had done the exact opposite. But that's the thing about the French. When they're being really nasty, they don't shout. They whisper. "You realize that I could have you arrested?" he asked.

I almost laughed. "What for?" I demanded.

"You were found in the middle of Paris,

full of drugs," the police chief explained. He sounded almost reasonable. "Two English tourists who decided to experiment with these forbidden substances..."

"THAT'S A COMPLETE LIE!" I exclaimed.

"YES!" Tim agreed. **"WE'RE NOT TOURISTS!"**

"And then there is the matter of the Bateau Mouche..." Moire continued. "You jumped off a bridge, endangering the lives of the people on the boat. This could also prove to be drug-related."

"What do you want, Moire?" I demanded.

Moire leaned forward. His face could have been carved out of stone. Even the cigarette smoke seemed to have solidified. "There are two things we wish to find out," he said. "First, who is the Mad American?"

"Why don't you ask Bastille and Lavache?" I demanded.

"They wouldn't tell us anything. And if we did arrest them, it would only let their boss know that we were getting close ... and that would ruin everything. The second thing we wish to know is, how are they smuggling the drugs across the Channel? As I have told you, we have searched the train many times ... but with no success. These packets of white powder – they must be somewhere. But..." He smacked his forehead with the palm of his hand. **"IT IS INFURIATING!"**

"What do you want us to do?" I asked.

"I want you to go back to the hotel," Moire replied. "It will be as if nothing has happened."

"Why?"

"Because you can be useful to me ... on the

inside. My men will continue to watch you. You'll be completely safe. But maybe you can find the answers to the questions. And if there is anything to report..."

"Forget it!" I snapped.

"Right!" Tim nodded. "Bestlé only paid for four days. We can't possibly afford it."

"Bestlé?" For the first time Moire looked puzzled. "Who is Bestlé?"

"It doesn't matter," I replied. "We're British citizens. You can't blackmail us!"

"You don't think so?" Moire almost smiled. "You are Europeans now, my friend. And if you don't do exactly as I tell you, let me assure you that you will be spending a great deal of time inside a European jail."

I wanted to argue, but I could see there was no point. The last person to argue with

Christien Moire probably found himself with a one-way ticket to Devil's Island.

He knew he'd beaten me. "Go back to Le Chat Gris and wait for further instructions," he said. "Don't worry about the bill. I will see to it."

"And what if we get killed?" I asked.

"My department will pay for the funeral too."

I sank back in my chair. There was nothing I could say. Not in French. Not in English. It really wasn't fair.

And that was how we found ourselves, a few hours later, back in our room at Le Chat Gris. As I'd walked back into the hotel, I'd known how those French aristocrats must have felt as they took their last steps towards the guillotine. The receptionist had almost fallen off his chair when he saw us and he'd been on the telephone before we'd reached the lift. The Mad American would have presumed we were dead. Now he'd know he was wrong. How long would it take him to correct his mistake?

Tim sat down on the bed. He was actually looking quite cheerful, which made me feel even worse. "Maybe this isn't so bad, Nick," he said.

"TIM!" I cried. **"HOW BAD CAN IT GET?"**

"We're working for the French police now," he said. "This could be good for business! *Tim Diamond Inc ... London and Paris.* That'll look good on the door."

"It'll look even better on your gravestone," I said. "Don't you understand, Tim?" We're not working for anyone! Christien Moire was lying through his teeth!"

"You mean ... he isn't a policeman?"

"Of course he's a policeman. But he doesn't want us to work for him. He's using us!" I'd taken a guidebook of Paris out of my case. Now I sat down next to Tim. "Moire wants to find out the identity of the Mad American," I explained. "What's the best way to do that?"

"Just ask for Tim Diamond..."

"Just *use* Tim Diamond. He's sent us back here because he knows that our turning up again will panic the Mad American. He's already tried to kill us twice. He's certain to try again – and this time Moire will be watching. He's using us as bait in a trap, Tim. The Mad American kills us. Moire gets the Mad American. It's as simple as that."

I opened the guidebook. "I'm not sitting here, waiting to be shot," I said.

"Where do you want to be shot?" Tim asked.

"I don't want to be shot anywhere! That's why I'm going to find the Mad American before he finds us." I started to thumb through the pages. I still didn't know what I was looking for, but I had a good idea. "After we were knocked out, we were taken to the Mad American's headquarters," I said.

"But we were knocked out!" Tim said. "We didn't see anything."

"We didn't see much," I agreed. "But there were some clues. A blue star. Some words in a shop window – **THE FRENCH CONFECTION**. And when we were tied up, I heard something. Music. Singing."

"Do you think that was the Mad American?"

"No, Tim. It was coming from a building nearby." I stopped, trying to remember what I had heard. "It wasn't French singing," I said. "It was different... It was foreign."

Sitting next to me on the bed, Tim was making a strange noise. I thought for a moment that he had stomach ache. Then I realized he was trying to hum the tune.

"That's right, Tim," I said. "It was something like that. Only a bit more human."

Tim stopped. I tried to think. How had the singing gone? It had been sad and somehow dislocated. A choir and a single male voice. At times it had been more like wailing than singing. Remembering it now made me think of a church. Was that it? Had it been religious music? But if so, what religion?

I'm not sure what happened first. The thought seemed to come into my mind at exactly the same moment as I found myself looking at the words *The Jewish Quarter* in the guidebook in my hands.

"Jewish music!" I exclaimed.

"Jewish?"

"The music that we heard, Tim. It was coming from a synagogue!"

Tim's eyes lit up. "You think we were taken to Jerusalem?"

"No, Tim. We were in Paris. But there's an area of Paris that's full of synagogues." I waved the book at him. "Le Marais. That's what it's called. The Jewish sector of Paris..."

"But how big is it?" Tim asked.

I read the page in front of me:

Originally a swamp, the Marais has grown to become one of the most fashionable areas of Paris. Its narrow streets are filled with shops and boutiques including some of the city's most elegant cafés and cake shops. The Marais is home to the Jewish quarter with numerous synagogues and kosher restaurants based around the Rue des Rosiers.

There was a map showing the area. It only had a couple of dozen roads. "It doesn't look too big," I said. "And at least we know what we're looking for. The French Confection."

"But what *is* The French Confection, Nick?"

"I think it must be a shop. Maybe it sells cakes or sweets or something. But once we've found it, we'll know we're right next to the factory. Find the sign and we'll have found the Mad American."

"And then?"

"Then we call Moire."

* * *

We slipped out of Le Chat Gris down the fire escape, dodging past Moire's men who were waiting for us at the front of the hotel. Then we dived into the nearest Metro station and headed north.

It was a short walk from the station to the start of Le Marais – the Place Vendôme, one of those Paris squares where even the trees manage to look expensive. From there we headed down towards a big, elegant building that turned out to be the Picasso museum. I'd studied Picasso at school. He's the guy who painted women with eyes in the sides of their necks and tables with legs going the wrong way. It's called surrealism. Maybe I should have taken Tim in, as he's pretty surreal himself. But we didn't have time.

We backtracked and found ourselves in a

series of long, narrow streets with buildings rising five storeys on both sides. But I knew we were on the right track. There was no singing, but here and there I saw blue stars – the same stars I had glimpsed as I was bundled into the van. I knew what it was now: the six-pointed Star of David. There was one in every kosher food store and restaurant in the area.

We'd been following the Rue des Rosiers – the one I'd read about in the guidebook – but with no sign of the building where we'd been held. So now we started snaking up and down, taking the first on the right and the next on the left and so on. It was a pretty enough part of Paris, I'll say that for it. Tim had even forgotten our mission and stopped once or twice to take photographs. We'd been chased and threatened at knife-point.

We'd been kidnapped, drugged and threatened again – this time by the French police. And he *still* thought we were on holiday!

And then, suddenly, we were there.

It was on one of the main streets of the area – the Rue de Sevigny. I recognized it at once: the burnt face of the building, the broken windows, the ugly chimney stacks... And there was the archway that we had driven through. There was a courtyard on the other side which was where the white van had been parked. I stood there in the sunlight, with people strolling past on the pavements, some carrying shopping bags, others pushing prams. And none of them knew. The biggest drug factory in Paris was right in front of them, just sitting there between a café and a cake shop, right in the middle of the Marais.

I couldn't believe I had found it so easily. It was hard to believe it was there at all.

"Nick...!" Tim whispered.

I grabbed hold of him and pulled him down behind a parked car as Bastille and Lavache appeared, coming out of the front door and walking across the courtyard. Each of them had a heavy box in their hands. Another shipment on its way out! It made me angry that anyone should be dumb enough to want to buy drugs and angrier still that these two grim reapers would be getting richer by selling them.

"What do we do now?" Tim whispered.

"Now we call Moire," I said.

"Right!" Tim straightened up. "Let's ask in there!"

Before I could stop him he had walked

across the pavement and into the cake shop. There was the sign in the window that I had seen from the van. **THE FRENCH CONFECTION**. Why did the name bother me? Why did I feel it was connected with something or someone I had seen? It was too late to worry about it now. Tim was already inside. I followed him in.

I found myself in a long, narrow shop with a counter running down one wall. Everywhere I looked there were cakes and croissants, bowls of coloured almonds and tiny pots of jam. The very air smelt of sugar and flour. On the counter stood one of the tallest wedding cakes I had ever seen: six platforms of swirly white icing with a marzipan bride and groom looking air-sick up on the top. There was a bead curtain at the back and now it rattled as the owner of the shop passed through, coming out to serve us. And of course I knew her. I'd met her on the train.

Erica Nice.

She stopped behind the counter, obviously as surprised to see us as we were to see her.

"You...!" she began.

"Mrs Nice!" Tim gurgled. I wondered how he had managed to remember her name. "We need to use your telephone. To call the police."

"I don't think so, Tim," I said.

Even as I spoke I was heading back towards the door. But I was already too late. Erica's hand came up and this time it wasn't holding an almond slice. It was the biggest gun I'd ever seen. Bigger than the wrinkled hand that held it. Its muzzle was as ugly as the smile on the old woman's face.

"But ... but ... but..." Tim stared.

"Erica Nice," I said. "I suppose I should have guessed. Madame Erica Nice. Say it fast and what do you get?"

"Madamericanice?" Tim suggested.

"Mad American," I said. "She's the one behind the drug racket, Tim. When we met her, she must have been checking the route. That's why she was on the train. And that's how Bastille and Lavache knew we were in Paris."

Erica Nice snarled at us. "Yes," she said. "I have to travel on the train now and then to keep an eye on things. Like that idiot steward – Marc Chabrol. He was scared. And scared people are no use to me."

"So you pushed him under a train," I said.

She shrugged. "I would have preferred to stab him. I did have my knitting needles, but unfortunately I was halfway through a woollen jumper. Pushing was easier."

"And what now?" I asked. I wondered if she

was going to shoot us herself or call her two thugs to finish the job for her. At the same time, I took a step forward, edging my way towards the counter and the giant wedding cake.

"Those idiots – Jacques and Luc – should have got rid of you when they had the chance," Erica hissed. "This time they will make no mistakes."

She turned to press a switch set in the wall. Presumably it connected the shop with the factory next door.

I leapt forward and threw my entire weight against the cake.

Erica half turned. The gun came up.

The door of the shop burst open, the glass smashing.

And as Erica Nice gave a single shrill scream and disappeared beneath about ten kilograms of wedding cake, Christien Moire and a dozen gendarmes hurled themselves into the shop. At the same time, I heard the blare of sirens as police cars swerved into the road from all directions.

I turned to Moire. "You followed us here?"

Moire nodded. "Of course. I had men on all sides of the hotel."

Erica Nice groaned and tried to fight her way out of several layers of sponge, jam and butter cream. Tim leaned forward and scooped up a fragment of white icing. He popped it into his mouth.

"Nice cake," he said.

The White Cliffs

The next day, Christien Moire drove us up to Calais and personally escorted us onto the ferry. It would have been easier to have taken the train, of course. But somehow Tim and I had had enough of trains.

It had been a good week for Moire. Jacques Bastille and Luc Lavache had both been arrested. So had Erica Nice. The drug factory had been closed down and more arrests were expected. No wonder Moire wanted us out of the way. He was looking forward to promotion and maybe the Croix de Guerre or whatever medal French heroes get pinned to their right nipple. The last thing Moire needed was Tim and me hanging around to tell people the part we had played.

Moire stopped at the quay and handed us our tickets as well as a packed lunch for the crossing. "France is in your debt," he said, solemnly, and before either of us could stop him he had grabbed hold of Tim and planted a kiss on both cheeks.

Tim went bright red. "I know I cracked the case," he muttered. "But let's not get too friendly..."

"It's just the French way," I said. Even so, I made sure I shook hands with Moire. I didn't want him getting too close.

"I wish you a good journey, my friends,"
Moire said. "And this time, perhaps you will
be careful what you say while you are on the
ship!"

"We won't be saying anything," I promised. I'd bought Tim a Tintin book at the
harbour bookstall. He could read that on
the way home.

Moire smiled. *"Au revoir,"* he said.

"Where?" Tim asked. I'd have to translate
it for him later.

We were about halfway home, this time chopping up and down on the Channel, when Tim suddenly looked up from the Tintin book. "You know," he said. "We never did find out how Erica Nice was smuggling the drugs on the train."

"Haven't you guessed?" I sighed and pulled out the blue sugar sachet that had started the whole thing. It was the sachet Tim had been given at the Gare du Nord. Somehow I'd never quite got round to opening it. I did so now.

There was a spoonful of white powder inside.

"Sugar?" Tim muttered.

"I don't think so, Tim," I replied. "This is just one sachet. But Erica Nice was transporting thousands of them every day on the train. A little parcel of drugs. One dose, already weighed and perfectly concealed." I tore open the packet and held it up. The powder was caught in the wind and snatched away. I watched it go, a brief flurry of white as it skimmed over the handrail and disappeared into the grey water of the English Channel.

"Do you think we ought to tell Moire?" Tim asked.

"I expect he's worked it out for himself," I said.

In the distance I could see the white cliffs of Dover looming up. We had only been away for a week but somehow it seemed a lot longer. I was glad to be home.

Tim was still holding the packed lunch that Moire had given us. Now he opened it.

The first thing he took out was a strawberry yoghurt.

"Very funny," I said.

The yoghurt followed the drugs into the channel. Then we went downstairs to order fish and chips.

The
GReeK
who STOLe
ChRiSTMaS

Death Threat

I knew it was going to be a bad Christmas when I walked past the charity shop and the manager ran out and tried to offer me charity. It seemed that everyone in Camden Town knew I was broke. Even the turkeys were laughing at me. On the last day of term, the teachers had a whip-round for me ... not that I really needed a whip, but I suppose it's the thought that counts. Christmas was just a few weeks away and the only money I had was a ten-pound book token that my parents had sent me from Australia. I tried to swap it for hard cash at my local bookshop, but the manager – a thin-faced woman in her forties – was completely heartless.

"I need to eat," I explained.

"Then buy a cookery book."

"I can't afford the ingredients!"

"I'm sorry. You can only use a book token to buy books."

"What's the point of buying books if I'm too faint to read?"

She smiled sadly at me. "Have you tried Philip Pullman?"

"No. Do you think he'd lend me some money?"

I couldn't believe my parents had sent me a book token for Christmas, but then of course they had no idea about anything. My dad had moved them to Sydney a few years before – he was a door-to-door salesman, selling doors, and he must have been doing well because this year he'd printed his own Christmas card. HAVE AN A-DOOR-ABLE CHRISTMAS, it said on the cover. There was a picture of a kangaroo with a red hat on, looking out of an open door. I was still laughing as I ripped it to pieces. My parents had two new kids of their own now: Doreen and Dora. Two sisters I'd never met. That made me sad sometimes. They weren't even two years old and they probably had more spare cash than me.

I was thinking about Australia as I walked home from the bookshop. My mum and dad had wanted to take me with them when they emigrated, and maybe it had been a mistake to slip off the plane before it took off. While it was taxiing down the runway, I was running away to find a taxi – and they hadn't even noticed until they were thirty-five thousand feet above France. Apparently my mum had hysterics. And my dad had my lunch.

I'm still not sure it was a smart decision. They say that London is like a village, and I certainly enjoyed living there. The only trouble was, I'd moved in with the village idiot. I'm talking, of course, about my big brother, Herbert Timothy Simple. But that wasn't what he called himself. He called himself Tim Diamond, Private Detective – and that's what it said in his advert, along with the line: "No problem too problematic." He'd written that himself.

Tim was the worst private detective in England. I mean ... he'd just spent two weeks working in a big department store in the West End. He was supposed to be looking out for shoplifters but I don't think he'd kept his eye on the ball. In fact, the ball was the first thing that got stolen. After that, things went from bad to worse. The store had twenty-three departments when he started but only sixteen when he left. He was fired, of course. The dummies in the window probably had a higher IQ than Tim. He was lucky he had me. I solved the crimes, Tim got the credit. That was how it worked. If you've read my other stories, you'll know what I'm talking about. If you haven't, go out and buy the books. If you like, I'll even sell you a ten-quid book token. You can have it for nine quid.

Anyway, right now Tim was out of work. And November had arrived like a bad dog, snapping at everyone in the street and sending them hurrying home. As usual, it wasn't going to snow – but the pipes were frozen, the puddles had iced over and you could see people's breath in the air.

They were playing a Christmas carol on the radio as I let myself in. Tim was sitting at his desk wrapped in a blanket, trying to open a tin of sardines that was so far past its sell-by date he'd probably have more luck selling it as an antique.

I threw myself into a chair. "Any news?" I asked. "I don't suppose anyone has offered you a job?"

"I just don't get it," Tim replied. "You'd think someone, somewhere would need a private detective. Why is no one hiring me?"

"Maybe it's because you're no good," I said.

"You might be right," Tim nodded sadly.

"There are police dogs that have solved more crimes than you."

"Yes," Tim agreed, "but at least I don't have fleas."

I got up and turned the radio off. Tim had managed to get the tin open and the room was suddenly filled with the smell of twenty-seven-year-old sardines. And it was just then that there was a knock on the door.

I looked at Tim. Tim looked at me. We had a client and we also had a room that looked like a rubbish tip and smelled like the River Thames during the Great Plague.

"ONE MINUTE!" Tim shouted.

In that one minute, we raced around like

two people in a speeded up commercial for Fairy Liquid. Papers went into drawers. Plates went into the kitchen. The sardines went into the bin and the bin went out the window. Sixty seconds later, the office looked more like an office and Tim was sitting behind his desk with a straightened tie and a crooked smile. I took one last look around and opened the door.

A man walked in. I guessed he was in his forties: short and fat, smoking a cigar. The cigar was short and fat too. He was dressed in a nasty suit. The pattern was so loud you could almost hear it coming. He had black, greasy hair, thick lips and eyes that would have been nicer if they'd matched. His shoes had been polished until you could see your face in them – though with his face I wouldn't have bothered. There was a gold signet ring on his finger. The way it squeezed the flesh, I doubted it would ever come off.

"You always keep your clients waiting outside?" he demanded as he came in and took a chair.

"We were filing," Tim explained.

He looked around. "I don't see no filing cabinets." He spoke like an American but he wasn't one. He was just someone who spent too much time on planes.

"We were filing our nails," I said.

He helped himself to one of Tim's business cards from the desk. "Are you Tim Diamond?"

"Yeah. That's me." Tim narrowed his eyes. He always does that when he's trying to look serious. Unfortunately it just makes him look short-sighted. "I'm a private eye."

"I know," the man growled. "That's why I'm here. My name is Jake Hammill and I want to hire you."

"You want to hire me?" Tim couldn't believe it. He leant forward. "So what can I do for you, Mr Camel?"

"Not Jay Camel. I'm Jake Hammill. You want me to spell it for you?"

"N-O," Tim said.

"I work in the music industry. As a matter of fact, I'm the manager of a woman who's a very famous pop singer."

Tim scowled. "If she's so famous, how come I've never heard of her?"

"I haven't told you her name yet."

"Maybe it would help if you did."

Hammill glanced at me. He was obviously suspicious. He turned back to Tim. "Can you keep a secret?" he asked.

"I'm not going to tell you," Tim replied.

"All right." Hammill nodded. "Her name is Minerva."

I have to admit, I was surprised. Hammill looked pretty small-time to me, but Minerva was one of the biggest names in the business. She was a multimillionaire pop singer and a movie actress. I doubted there was anyone in the world who hadn't seen her music videos. She was the woman with the golden voice and the silver-plated breasts. Her clothes were out-rageous – like the rest of her lifestyle. She had been born in Greece but now she lived most of the time in New York. The fact that she was visiting London had made the front page of every newspaper ... even the *Financial Times*.

"The thing is," Hammill said, "I've got a serious problem..." He twisted his signet ring nervously around his finger like he was trying to take it off. "Listen to me," he went on. "Minerva has been invited over here for Christmas. Tomorrow she's turning on the Christmas lights in Regent Street.

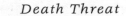

And on Thursday at midday she's opening the Santa Claus grotto at Harrods department store in Knightsbridge. There's going to be a lot of press. A lot of TV. It's great publicity. But this is the problem..." He drew a breath. "I think she's in danger."

"What makes you think that?" I asked.

"Well, yesterday she received an anonymous letter."

"An anonymous letter!" Tim exclaimed. "Who from?"

Hammill scowled. "I don't know. It was anonymous. But it threatens her with death."

"So where is this letter, Mr Hubble?" Tim asked.

"It was sent to Minerva. She's got it. I'd like

you to come and meet her at her hotel and she'll take you through it."

"She'll take me through the hotel?"

"No. She'll take you through the letter." He leant forward and already I could see the doubt in his face. "I have to say, Mr Diamond, I need to be sure you're the right man for this job. I wanted to go to the police, but Minerva's husband insisted that a private detective would be better. I looked you up on Google."

That's right, put the word "idiot" into any search engine and Tim's name will come up.

"I take it you know how to look after your-self," Hammill said.

Tim looked puzzled. "But I'm not ill!" he muttered.

Hammill rolled his eyes. Maybe I was imagining things but I could have sworn they went in opposite directions. "I'm not asking about your health," he said. "I need someone to stay close to Minerva while she's in London, and that may mean getting into a fight. So what I'm asking you is – do you know judo or karate?"

"Sure!" Tim nodded. "Judo, karate and origami. When do you want me to start, Mr Rubble?"

It was obvious to me that Hammill was having second thoughts about Tim. And maybe third and fourth thoughts too. For a moment he bit his fingernail, deep in thought. Maybe he had plans to bite all the way down to the signet ring. Then he came to a decision. "All right," he said. "Minerva is staying at the Porchester hotel, which is in Hyde Park. That's highly confidential information by the way."

"What do you mean?" Tim demanded. "Everyone knows that the Porchester hotel is in Hyde Park."

"Sure. But nobody knows she's staying there. Otherwise we'd have fans all over the place."

"That would help with the ventilation..."

"Minerva likes her privacy. She's booked in under the name of Mrs Smith. Room sixteen. I want you to visit her this evening. Say, seven o'clock?"

"Seven o'clock," Tim said obediently.

"That's right. I'll let her take a look at you and if she thinks you're up to it, you're hired."

Tim nodded. I knew what was coming next. He was sitting back in his chair with his feet resting on his desk, trying to look every inch the private detective. The fact that he had a hole in one of his shoes didn't help. As far as he was concerned he was back in business. And he was determined to prove it. "What about my fee?" he demanded.

"You're not hired yet," Hammill reminded him.

"OK, Mr Rabble. But I'd better let you know now, I'm not cheap. The only thing that goes cheap in this office is my budgerigar, and I don't think your superstar wants a body-guard with feathers."

Hammill tried to make sense of this, decided it wasn't worth trying and stood up. "I'll see you this evening," he said. One last twist of the ring. It wasn't going anywhere, but he was. He walked out of the office, slamming the door behind him.

There was a moment's silence.

I went over to the cupboard and searched through the CDs. I knew we'd have a Minerva recording somewhere and, sure enough, there it was – her third album, *Think Pink*. I looked at the face on the cover: the blonde hair, the green eyes, the lips that looked like they could suck in a horse. It was strange really that we still had CD's when the whole world was downloading its music. On the other hand, we no longer had a CD player. Tim had thrown it out months ago ... along with just about everything else that no longer had a use. That was another sad thought. When I walked past the local skip, it looked more like home than home did.

But maybe our luck was going to change. All Tim had to do was protect her for a couple of days and there'd be a handsome cheque at the end of it. He might even end up taking a bullet for her. If so, I just hoped they'd pay him extra. And whatever happened, it might be fun to hang out with one of the biggest entertainers on the planet.

"I can't believe it!" I said. "We're going to meet Minerva!"

"It's even better than that," Tim replied. "She's opening the grotto at Harrods. Maybe we'll meet Father Christmas!"

I slid the CD back into the cupboard.

Minerva had just received a death threat and her husband had hired Tim Diamond. That was like getting her a knitted cardigan when what she really needed was a bullet-proof vest. Well, one thing was certain: this was going to be a Christmas to remember. I just wondered if Minerva would still be around to see in the New Year.

Suite Sixteen

The Porchester was in the middle of London's Park Lane, a five-star hotel that cost the earth. The sort of place I wouldn't be able to stay in a blue moon. You could tell it was expensive: I spotted two celebrities in the revolving doors and by the time I'd reached the reception desk I'd passed three more. There was enough fur and jewellery in that place to fill a store. And that was just the men.

The reception area was all glass and marble, including the receptionist's dress. That's fashion for you. Tim and I had arrived half an hour early to drink in the atmosphere – and looking at the prices in the hotel bar we certainly weren't going to be drinking anything else. A glass of water here cost the same as a glass of wine anywhere else, and for a glass of wine you needed to take out a loan. Nothing cost peanuts here ... not even the peanuts. That's the thing about the super-rich. They don't mind when things are crazily expensive. It just reminds them how rich they are.

We went over to the reception desk and asked to see "Mrs Smith". The receptionist was a slinky-looking girl with long fingernails. She had perfect teeth but she didn't smile and she spoke through her nose, so I guessed she didn't like showing them. She picked up a telephone and dialled a number with a fingernail that was a little longer than her finger. She spoke for a few seconds, then put the phone down. Her earrings jangled. So did my nerves.

"The second floor," she said, barely moving her lips. Maybe she was training to be a ventriloquist. "It's suite sixteen."

So Minerva had a suite, not a single room. We took the lift to the second floor and I have to admit I enjoyed the journey. It's the only lift I've ever seen with solid gold buttons and a chandelier. I could see Tim staring at everything as if he'd just died and gone to heaven. He'd insisted on putting on a suit, which he'd found at the bottom of the wardrobe. It was just a shame that the moths had found it first.

Still, so long as nobody wondered why the jacket had seventeen buttonholes but only seven buttons, he'd be fine.

The lift door opened and we found ourselves in a corridor with about a mile of pink carpet, more chandeliers and the sort of wallpaper that seemed wasted on a wall. Suite sixteen was about halfway down – a double wooden door with gold numbers on.

Tim raised his hand, about to knock. And that was when we heard it. A sudden, loud crack from the other side. A gunshot? I wasn't so sure but Tim had no doubt at all. His eyes widened and he threw himself at the door – shoulder-first – obviously intending to smash it down, climb through the wreckage and rescue Minerva from whoever was taking pot shots at her. It didn't budge. Tim howled as he dislocated his shoulder. I reached out and opened the door. It was unlocked anyway.

We ran in. The door led straight into a plush living room. There were three people there. One of them was Jake Hammill, the manager who had come to our office that afternoon. The other was an older man dressed in a velvet jacket with a silk cravat around his neck. He had one of those permanent suntans that give your skin the colour of a peach but the texture of a prune. The third was Minerva. I recognized her at once with that strange buzz of excitement you get when you find yourself face to face with someone really famous. She was holding half a Christmas cracker. The tanned man was holding the other half. Well, that explained the bang we had just heard.

"Who the hell are you?" the older man asked.

"I'm Tim Diamond." Tim shrugged and I heard a loud click as his shoulder blade somehow managed to slip back into place. Well, that was something. Minerva looked as if she was about to call the police. At least she wouldn't have to ask for an ambulance too.

"So what do you mean just bursting in

here?" the man continued. "Haven't you ever heard of knocking?"

"Wait a minute! Wait a minute!" Hammill interjected. "This is the private detective I was telling you about. The one you told me to see. Tim Diamond."

"What about the kid?" the man asked.

"I'm his little brother, Nick," I said.

"Yeah, well ... you'd better sit down."

Minerva had been watching all this with a mixture of puzzlement and disbelief. I sat down on the sofa next to her, thinking that a million kids would have given their right arm to be where I was right now and wondering what she'd do with a million right arms. She was dressed simply in expensive jeans and a white shirt, but even so she was one of the most beautiful women I'd ever seen. She had long, blonde hair, eyes that were somewhere between blue and green and the sort of body that made me wish I was older than fourteen. Maybe she was smaller than I'd imagined but then I don't have much imagination. And looking at her, I didn't need it. She was the real thing and she was right there next to me.

Meanwhile, Tim had sat down in a chair. I could tell he fancied Minerva too. As far as I know, Tim has never had a steady girlfriend. He just simply hasn't had any luck finding a woman who's attracted to a twenty-eight-year-old with no money and no brains. To be fair to Tim, he's not that unattractive. I mean, he's slim and he's dark and he's reasonably fit. And it seemed to me that Minerva was definitely interested in him. Mind you, if the old, wrinkled guy was her husband, I wasn't that surprised. How did a world-famous sex symbol end up married to her grandfather?

"So – how can I help you?" Tim asked with a lazy smile. He crossed one leg over the other and his foot caught a lamp, sending the shade flying.

"I told you," Hammill growled. "Minerva needs a bodyguard."

"With a body like that I'm not surprised!" Tim agreed.

"HOLD ON!" the old man interrupted. "That's my wife you're talking about."

"And who are you?" Tim asked.

"I'M HER HUSBAND!" He was perched on the arm of the sofa next to Minerva. "My name is Harold Chase." He lay a hand on Minerva's shoulder, and maybe I was wrong but I could have sworn she shuddered slightly.

"I'm paying you to make sure nobody hurts my baby."

"You've got a baby?" Tim demanded.

"I'm talking about Minerva!"

"I don't need looking after," Minerva said. They were the first words she had spoken, and I could hear the faint Greek accent fighting to get out. I was also reminded that this was the voice that had sold millions of albums. "I don't need looking after"; it almost sounded like the title of one of her songs.

"We've got to take control of this situation," Hammill cut in. "You read what that letter said. Show it to Mr Diamond."

Minerva thought for a moment, then pulled a white envelope out of her pocket. She held it for a moment. "This arrived yesterday," she said. "It was slipped under the door of my suite. It's from somebody who hates me."

Tim opened the letter and read aloud:

DEAR MINERVA, YOU ARE A MONSTER. I CANNOT FOREGIVE YOU FOR WHAT YOU DID IN TROPOJË LAST SUMMER. HOW COULD YOU DO THAT? I WILL NEVER FORGET IT AND VERY SOON I AM GOING TO KILL YOU. YOUR LIFE WILL COME TO AN END IN LONDON. THIS WILL BE YOUR LAST CHRISTMAS!

Tim lowered the letter. "What makes you think that whoever wrote this hates you?" he asked.

Minerva stared at him. "I'm sorry?" she quavered.

"Well, he does call you *dear* Minerva..."

I snatched up the letter. It was straight out of a computer: blue ink on a plain sheet of paper. I noticed that whoever had written it couldn't spell "forgive". The envelope was addressed: Minerva, Suite 16.

"What happened in Tropojë?" I asked.

"Nothing happened in Tropojë," Harold replied.

"It's the concert," Hammill cut in. "It's gotta be!"

"Forget it, Jake."

"No, Harry. They might as well know." Hammill turned to us. "It was just one of those things," he explained. "It happened last summer, like the letter says. Minerva was going to give a big charity concert in Albania. It was to benefit OAK."

"What's OAK?"

"Overweight Albanian Kids. It tries to help kids who watch too much TV and eat too many McDonald's. Some of them have to wear elasticized clothing. Many of them are in wheelchairs. They can walk – they're just too lazy. Anyway, they were really looking forward to the concert, but at the last moment Minerva had to pull out."

"Why?" I asked.

"I had a headache," Minerva replied. Obviously the overweight kids of OAK had never given her much cause for concern. Until now.

"You upset a lot of fans, Minerva," Jake said.

"And you think one of the fans is out to get her?"

"That's what it looks like."

I wasn't so sure. The idea of an oversized Albanian TV addict travelling all the way to

England to kill Minerva sounded a bit far-fetched to me. On the other hand, there was that spelling mistake: English clearly wasn't their first language. But there was something about the letter I didn't like – and I don't just mean the death threat. I knew there was something wrong. Something didn't add up. But I hadn't yet had time to work out what it was.

"My own feeling is that we should just get out of London," the husband said. "I can't sleep with the thought of you being in danger."

"Harold – you're exaggerating!" Minerva shook her head. "This trip is great publicity. Turning on the lights and opening the grotto is a big deal. I'm not going to run away just because some freak writes me a stupid letter." She turned to Tim. "I've got a single coming out on December twenty-fifth," she said.

"What's it called?" I asked.

Tim sighed. "It's called Christmas Day, Nick," he said. "Everyone knows that."

"I mean – what's the single called?"

"It's a song about cowboys," Minerva said. "The title is 'Like a Virginian'." She fell silent for a moment and then she really surprised me. "If you boys are going to work with me, you might as well know that I hate this god-damn country and I hate Christmas."

"Minerva—" Harold began.

"Shut up, Harold! I just want to put my cards on the table."

"Your Christmas cards?" Tim asked.

"I don't have any. Those stupid pictures of angels and three wise men. If they were so wise, what was all that business with the gold, frankincense and myrrh? You think a baby's

got any use for that sort of stuff?"
She shook her head. "I hate
everything about Christmas.
Those stupid Christmas trees
that drop needles all over the
carpet. Those boring carols that go on and
on. Santa Claus with his stupid beard."

"What about Christmas presents?" I asked.

"Why would I care about Christmas presents? I've got everything I want already." She
realized she was still holding the half-cracker
that she had pulled with her husband when we
came in. "And I don't like these stupid crackers either," she went on. "They were sent up
to the room by some fan or someone and all
they've given me is a headache. As far as I'm
concerned, the best thing to do with Christmas would be to forget the whole thing."

She threw down the cracker. A silver acorn and a slip of paper rolled out onto the table.

I don't know what it was that made me pick up the piece of paper. Maybe after Minerva's little speech I needed a laugh. Or maybe there was something about it that whispered to me that actually it didn't belong in a cracker. Anyway, I unfolded it and sure enough there was the same blue ink as the letter, the same typeface. There were just two lines:

```
WHEN MINERVA SEES THE LIGHTS
THAT'S WHEN I'LL HAVE HER IN MY SIGHTS
```

I read it out.

"I don't get it," Tim said. "It's not very funny..."

"IT'S NOT A JOKE, TIM!" I exclaimed. "It's another death threat."

"BUT THAT'S IMPOSSIBLE!" Harold seized the piece of paper and held it with a shaking hand. "How did this get inside the cracker?" he demanded. He stared at Jake Hammill. "You brought them up here!" he continued accusingly. "What's going on?"

"I just picked them up from reception!" Hammill replied. "They said they'd been left in your name by a fan."

"What does it mean?" Minerva asked. Her voice had gone quiet.

Nobody spoke – so I did. "It must mean tomorrow," I said. "When you turn on the Christmas lights." I picked up the acorn. It was heavy – solid silver, maybe.

"And look at this," I said.

"An acorn..." Tim was puzzled.

"Off an *oak* tree, Tim," I said. "They're telling you who it came from."

"Of course!" Harold Chase stood up. He was shaking so much, I was worried something was going to fall off. "That's it," he said. "We're not going to turn on the lights. Forget it. We're not going anywhere near them."

"Harold..." Hammill began.

"I mean it, Jake."

"Forget it, Harold!" Minerva had also got to her feet. "Look – I've already promised. I'm going to turn on these stupid lights. I've got to be there: the Mayor of London is coming. All the press will be out. It's going to be a big event."

"It'll be an even bigger event if someone shoots you," I muttered.

Tim turned to me. "That's a terrible thing to say, Nick!" He thought for a moment. "Anyway, they might not shoot her. They might run her over or blow her up or possibly fix the wires so she gets electrocuted..."

Minerva had gone a little pale. "Do you think you can protect me, Mr Diamond?" she asked.

Tim smiled. "I'm the private eye who never blinks," he replied. "And from this moment I'm not going to let you out of my sight. I'm going to walk with you, eat with you and go to bed with you—"

"Hey! Wait a minute! I'm in the bed!" Harold interrupted.

"We have a four-poster," Minerva said.

"That's great," Tim said. "We can have one post each."

Jake Hammill stepped forward. "I think Minerva will be safe enough while she's here at the Porchester hotel," he said. "Suppose Mr Diamond joins us tomorrow evening on the way to Regent Street?"

Minerva nodded. "I'm staying in all day tomorrow. That'll be fine."

"That just leaves the question of your fee, Mr Diamond," Hammill continued.

"No question about it," Tim said. "I want one."

"Of course." Hammill blinked uncertainly. "We'll pay you two hundred pounds a day. But let's get one thing straight. If anyone takes a shot at Minerva, we'll expect you to step in front of the bullet."

"Don't worry!" Tim jerked a thumb at me. "That's what he's for."

So there it was, signed and sealed. I still wondered why Minerva hadn't gone straight to the police – but maybe it wouldn't suit her being surrounded by the men in blue. I wanted to tell her that Tim would offer her about as much protection as a paper umbrella in the rain, but two hundred pounds was two hundred pounds. I watched as Jake Hammill counted out the money, and it occurred to me that the only time I'd been expecting to see the Queen that Christmas had been on her TV broadcast. But here were twenty little portraits sliding into Tim's outstretched hand. I almost wanted to kiss her. Or him.

We took the bus home. We could have afforded a cab but we'd already decided to blow a big chunk of the money on a three-course meal at our local Italian. I was already dreaming of a twelve-inch pizza on an eleven-inch plate. Extra cheese and pepperoni. And maybe extra pizza too. But even so, I couldn't get Minerva out of my mind. I went over what had happened in the suite. I was still certain something was wrong.

"If you ask me, Tim, there's something strange about this," I said.

Tim looked around him. "It's just a bus, Nick," he said.

"I'm not talking about the bus. I'm talking about Minerva. Those death threats! Whoever heard of a death threat inside a Christmas cracker?"

"Yeah," Tim nodded. "And there was no sign of a paper hat."

I shook my head. "I wouldn't be surprised if they weren't making the whole thing up ...

the three of them. You heard what she said. All she wants to do is sell her new album. Maybe the whole thing's just a publicity stunt."

Tim shook his head. "I don't think so, Nick. I think she's in real danger. Don't ask me why – I've just got an instinct for this sort of thing. A sixth sense."

"Sure," I muttered. "It's just a shame you missed out on the other five."

I looked out of the window. It had got dark a while ago and it looked as if it was going to snow. There were a few flakes dancing in the wind. As we turned a corner, I noticed a man standing on the pavement with a sandwich board. He was handing out leaflets about the end of the world. London is full of people like that. Maybe it's the city that drives them mad or maybe they're mad before they arrive and it's the city that attracts them. Anyway, this man had three words in red paint across his chest:

DEATH WILL COME

He seemed to catch my eye as we went past. And I found myself wondering. Was he just a harmless crank trying to sell religion to anyone who would listen?

Or did he know something I didn't?

Regent Street

Everyone makes a fuss about the Christmas lights on Regent Street and maybe there was a time when they were actually worth travelling in to see. I remember when I was small, my mum would take me into town and the lights would flicker and flash and sparkle and people would cross the road with their necks craned, staring at them in wonderment, and they wouldn't even complain when they were run over by the 139 bus.

But that was then. Nowadays the lights are more or less the same as they are on any other high street at Christmas. Worse than that, they're paid for by big business, so you don't just get Santa, stars or whatever. You get the latest characters from a Disney movie. Or "Harry Christmas" from J.K. Rowling. Or whatever.

Even so, turning on the lights is still a big deal. If it isn't a member of the royal family, it's a pop star or a Hollywood actor. All the newspapers and TV stations record the moment when the button gets pressed, and the next day you can read all about it on page one: **MINERVA LIGHTS UP LONDON**. And just for one day the earthquakes and the wars and the dirty politics are left to page two.

We were driven to Regent Street in a

stretch limo. The chauffeur was a tall, slim man in a grey uniform and I couldn't help wondering if someone hadn't stretched him too. Minerva and her husband sat on the back seat. For the first time I noticed he was wearing a hearing aid, but he didn't need it because no one was talking to him. She was gazing out of the window. It was made from special glass so that no one could look in. Her manager, Jake Hammill, had the next seat to himself. Tim and I were closest to the front – and furthest from the bar. The three of them were drinking champagne but all we'd been offered was a glass of iced water. Well, we were staff. Official security and its younger brother.

As usual Minerva was in a bad mood, but I had to admit that from where I was sitting she looked fabulous. She was wearing a bright red number with white fur trimmings. Think Father Christmas only thirty years younger and after major cosmetic surgery. Her lips were bright red too, shaped like a perfect kiss. It would have been hard to believe that this was the woman who hated Christmas. She'd done herself up like the sort of present every man in London would want to open. I glanced at Tim and saw that he was drooling. I just hoped it wouldn't stain the carpet.

"Now, remember!" Harold Chase said to his wife. She turned round slowly and looked at him without a lot of interest. "You pose for the cameras. You make a little speech. You turn on the lights. And then we get the hell out of there."

"What's the big worry?" Minerva drawled.

"The big worry?" Harold's eyes bulged. For a nasty minute I thought they were going to fall out of his face. "There could be a killer out there, baby. You're going to be out in the open, exposed. Anyone could take a shot at you." He leant forward and turned to Tim. "You'd better keep your eyes open, Mr Diamond," he said.

"You don't have to worry, Mr Cheese," Tim assured him. "I've had my eyes on your wife all evening."

"Well, you'd just better make sure nothing goes wrong."

"What could possibly go wrong with me around?" Tim exclaimed. He threw his hands back in a gesture of surprise, emptying his glass of iced water over the driver.

The car drew to a halt. It was just coming

up to six o'clock on a cold, dry Tuesday evening, but the shops were still open and there were Christmas shoppers everywhere. We got out and suddenly the night seemed to explode in a thousand flashes. They came so thick and fast that I found myself blinded. It was as if I had entered an electrical storm that signalled the end of the world.

Of course, it was nothing so dramatic. Minerva was being photographed by a huge pack of press photographers, all of them holding up great, chunky cameras with lenses that were definitely pleased to see her. For a few seconds Minerva seemed to be frozen, half in the car and half out of it. Then she came to her senses and began to smile and wave; the silent, bad-tempered woman who had been sitting opposite me was instantly replaced by the perfect star that she was as the lights flashed all around her. And at that moment I got an idea of what it must be like to be a celebrity – loved not because of what you are but because of what the cameras want you to be.

At the same time, I was puzzled. Minerva had received two death threats. Even if she had decided not to take them seriously, her husband and manager had been worried enough to hire Tim and me. And yet here she was completely surrounded by photographers. It occurred to me that any one of them could have a gun. There were a few police around, but right now killing Minerva would be the easiest thing in the world. I said nothing. I could only stand there as she turned and smiled and smiled and turned while the photographers shouted at her from every side.

"OVER HERE, MINERVA!"

"GIVEUSASMILE, MINERVA!"

"THISWAY, MINERVA!"

Tim nudged me. He was standing with his back to the car, blinking in the flashlights, but I could see that he was suddenly alert. I followed his eyes and saw a rather shabby-looking man in a suit hurrying towards us and suddenly I knew what was going to happen.

"Leave this to me..." Tim muttered.

"No, Tim!" I began.

But it was too late. Tim charged forward and grabbed hold of the man, then spun him around and threw him onto the bonnet of the limousine.

"THAT'S FAR ENOUGH!" Tim exclaimed.

"I... I... I..." The man was too shocked to speak.

"What do you want with Minerva?" Tim demanded.

"I'M THE MAYOR OF LONDON!" the man exclaimed.

Tim looked suspicious. He was still pinning him down. "If you're the Mayor of London, where's your red cloak and pointy hat?"

"I'm not that sort of mayor," the man growled. "I think you've been watching too many pantomimes."

"Oh no I haven't!" Tim replied.

By now, two policemen had appeared and had pulled Tim away, helping the Mayor to his feet. Because it *was* the Mayor, of course. I'd recognized him instantly – his bald head, his brightly coloured cheeks and his entirely colourless moustache. Jake Hammill had seen what had happened. He hurried over and placed himself between the Mayor and Tim.

"I'm so sorry!" he said. "We've hired private security and I guess he was a little jumpy."

"It's an outrage," the Mayor exclaimed. He had a whiny voice.

"Come and meet Minerva, Mr Mayor. She's been longing to say hello."

The thought of shaking Minerva's hand – or indeed any part of her – must have cheered the Mayor up because he seemed to have forgotten that he had just been attacked by Tim. Hammill took him over to his client, who was still posing for the cameras. "Minerva ... this is the Mayor!" he said.

"How lovely to meet you, Mr Mayor!" Minerva sounded so genuine, I almost believed her myself. She kissed him on the cheek and night became day again as the photographers captured the moment for the morning's headlines. "Where do we go to turn on the lights?" she asked.

"This way..." The Mayor had gone red.

We made our way to a raised platform that had been constructed at the side of the road. There must have been four or five hundred people all around us, many of them waving autograph books and flashing cameras of their own. A Salvation Army band was playing carols. They finished "Away in a Manger" and began a version of "Silent Night" that was anything but.

Minerva climbed the stairs and I couldn't stop myself thinking of gallows and public hangings. I remembered the warning inside the cracker. Was someone really about to have a crack at her? I tried to think where I would hide myself if I were a sniper. I looked up at the rooftops. It was hard to see anything in the darkness but there didn't seem to be anyone there. How about an open window? All the windows in the street were closed. Then perhaps in the crowd...

By now Minerva had reached the top of the stairs. Was she being brave or stupid? Or was it just that she refused to take any of this seriously?

Jake Hammill was certainly looking nervous. So was Harold Chase. He was standing to one side, his hands in his pockets, pulling his black cashmere coat around him like he was trying to hide in it. His eyes were darting left and right. Even if nobody took a shot at his wife, I'd have said a major heart attack was a strong possibility. He didn't look like he'd last the night.

So there we all were on the platform: Minerva and the Mayor at the front, the rest of us grouped behind. There was a single red button, mounted on a wooden block, and a microphone. Minerva stepped forward. The crowd fell silent. The Salvation Army players came to the end of a verse and stopped – unfortunately not all at the same time.

"LADIES AND GENTLEMEN!" It was the Mayor speaking. His voice whined the full length of Regent Street and it wasn't just the fault of the microphone. "I'd like to welcome you all here and I hope you've all remembered to pay the congestion charge! We've had some great stars turn on the lights in Regent Street. But this year, if you ask me, we've got the biggest star of all. Please welcome ... **MINERVA!**"

Everyone clapped and cheered.

"Thank you. Thank you so very much!" Minerva's voice echoed after the Mayor's. "I'm so thrilled to be here, at Christmas. It's such a wonderful time of the year – the birth of baby Jesus and of course my new single is about to be released. So Happy Christmas to everyone, and here goes..."

She lifted her finger.

And that was when it happened.

There were two gunshots. They sounded incredibly close and there could be no doubt that Minerva was the target. At once the entire atmosphere changed. There was a single second of frozen silence and then screams as the crowd panicked and began to scatter, people pushing each other to get out of the way. The band was swept away in the stampede. I saw someone fall into the big drum. The cymbal player was knocked off her feet with a final crash. On the platform, the Mayor had been the first to dive for cover. Minerva hadn't moved, as if unsure what to do. I couldn't see if she had been hit or not. With that bright red dress, it was hard to tell.

Then Tim leapt into action. I have to hand it to him – at least he was braver than the Mayor, who had curled into a ball in the corner of the platform with his head buried in his hands. Tim had been hired to protect Minerva and that was what he was going to do – even if the shots had already been fired. Even if she was already dead.

"GET DOWN!" he shouted.

He lunged forward and I guessed that he meant to throw himself on top of Minerva – which, I had to admit, was quite an attractive idea. Unfortunately, Minerva had already stepped aside. Tim missed and landed, with his arms outstretched, on the red button.

At once, ten thousand light bulbs burst into multi-coloured life. This year the

Regent Street lights had been sponsored by McDonald's. They depicted stars and Christmas trees decorated with twinkling hamburgers and fries. At the same time, a specially arranged Christmas carol – "We Wish You a McMerry Christmas" – boomed out of the speakers.

The Mayor opened one eye. **"YOU IDIOT!"** he screamed. **"YOU'VE TURNED ON THE CHRISTMAS LIGHTS INSTEAD OF MINERVA!"**

I'm not sure what would have happened next. Perhaps Tim would have ended up being murdered himself. But then Harold Chase stepped forward and pointed. **"THERE!"** he yelled. **"THERE HE IS!"**

He was pointing at the rooftops and now, with all the extra bulbs burning below, the darkness had become a sea of red and blue and yellow and white. And sure enough, high above one of the department stores, I could make out a short, plump figure half-hidden behind a chimney stack. He was staring down at us and, although I couldn't see what it was from this distance, there was definitely something in his hand. A gun? He certainly would have had a clear shot at Minerva from where he was standing – but not any more. Half a dozen policemen had already reached the platform and they had all grabbed a piece of her. Jake and Harold were also grabbing at her. Tim had crawled off the red button and was trying to climb on top. The entire platform looked like a training session for the All Blacks with Minerva in the middle of the scrum.

The figure on the roof didn't seem to be

moving and that was when I decided to take action. I didn't really know what I was doing. Part of me was asking questions. Why hadn't I seen the sniper earlier? Why hadn't he made a faster escape – or at least tried to fire off a few more shots? Was that a gun in his hand? And part of me knew that I wouldn't find the answers hanging around on Regent Street. I had to go and look for them myself.

I leapt down from the platform, pushed my way through what was left of the crowd and plunged into the nearest shop. It was a huge place selling clothes that I couldn't possibly afford and – one glance told me – that I wouldn't want to buy if I could. Blue blazers and red cravats have never been my style. There was a lift opposite the front door and I was lucky. The doors were just closing as I arrived. I ran in and pressed the top button – the sixth floor. I was lucky again. The lift didn't stop on the way up.

The sixth floor seemed to be devoted to Christmas presents for people you don't like: really nasty golfing jumpers, oversized umbrellas and multicoloured shoes. There weren't too many shoppers around as I burst out of the lift and made for the nearest fire door. Sure enough, a flight of concrete stairs led up to the roof. I took them two at a time and it only occurred to me now that I was unarmed and about to come face to face with a would-be assassin who probably wouldn't be too pleased to see me. But it was too late to go back. And, I figured, he couldn't be more deadly than those golfing jumpers.

I reached a door marked FIRE EXIT and

slammed into it ... which, incidentally, set off all the fire alarms and the sprinkler system on the seven floors below. But now I was on the roof: a strange landscape of chimneys, satellite dishes, water tanks and air-conditioning units. I stopped for a moment and let my eyes get used to the darkness. Not that it was exactly pitch black. The Regent Street lights were still glittering below me and, looking down, I could see the scattered crowds, the police, what was left of the Salvation Army band.

Something moved. And there he was, the man that Harold Chase had seen from below. He was only about fifteen metres away from me, cowering on the other side of the roof. He didn't look like your typical assassin. He was short and very fat – almost spherical – with white, curly hair. I wondered if he was one of the overweight Albanians. It was Minerva's absence at a concert in Albania that had started all this.

The man looked at me with something between horror and dismay. He raised a hand as if to prevent me moving forward.

"NO!" he shouted. "I d-d-didn't..."

Then he turned and ran.

I chased after him and that was when I discovered that I had miscalculated. I had run into the wrong store and there was a three-metre gap between his roof and mine. But I hadn't come this far to let an impossible jump and a probable fall to my death seven floors below worry me. I picked up speed and threw myself off the edge.

For a moment I hung in the air and I could feel the ground a very long way beneath me.

The cold night air was rushing into me and – for a nasty moment – so was the pavement. The other roof was too far away. I wasn't going to make it. Suddenly I was angry with myself. Who did I think I was? Spider-Man? If so, I'd forgotten to pack a web.

But I didn't fall. Somehow my outstretched hands caught hold of the edge of the other roof and I winced as my stomach and shoulders slammed into the brickwork. I could taste blood and dust in my mouth. I'd cut my lip and maybe loosened a couple of my teeth. Using what little strength I had left, I managed to pull myself up and roll to safety. Painfully, I got to my feet. I wasn't surprised to see that the little fat man had gone.

He had left something behind. I saw them – three small silver objects on the asphalt.

At first I thought they were bullets, but as I walked towards them, I realized they were too big. People down in the street were pointing up at me and shouting as I dropped to one knee and scooped them into my hand.

Three oak leaves. That was what the sniper had left behind. The acorn in the cracker and now this. He was definitely trying to tell me something and I'd got the message loud and clear.

Dinner for Two

When I woke up the next morning, we were right back where we'd started. Which is to say, we were in Camden Town, in the office, and once again Tim was out of work. It turned out that nobody had been particularly impressed by my death-defying leap when all I'd got to show for it was grazed arms, bruises and a handful of silver oak leaves. I'd given the police a description of the man I'd seen on the roof – not that it added up to much. Small and fat. The curly hair could have been a wig. And although he had spoken, he hadn't said enough for me to be sure whether he had an Albanian accent or not.

As I'd sat in the bath that night, I'd gone over his words a dozen times. *No! I d-d-didn't...* Had he been scared or did he always stammer like that? And what had he meant? The police had decided that he was angry – that he was telling me he hadn't shot Minerva in the sense that he had missed. To me it seemed simpler than that. "I didn't do it. It wasn't me." That was what he had been trying to say. But then why had he left the oak leaves behind? Maybe they were the symbol of the society for Overweight Albanian Kids. And finally, where was the gun? I thought

I'd seen something in his hand but he hadn't had it when I reached the roof.

Anyway, the case was over as far as we were concerned. Now that the police knew Minerva was in real danger, they had taken over protection duties – and looking at some of those officers leering at her on Regent Street, I could see that plenty of them were going to be putting in for overtime. The good news was that we still had about seventy pounds of the two hundred Jake Hammill had given us. That would buy us a Christmas turkey, Brussels sprouts, roast potatoes and chestnut stuffing. It was just a shame that Tim had sold the oven.

I found him at breakfast with a bowl of cornflakes and the morning newspaper. He wasn't looking too pleased and I soon saw why. He'd made the front page. There was a picture of him spread out on his stomach just after he had accidentally turned on the Christmas lights.

"Have you seen this?" he wailed as I sat down. "And look at this!"

He tapped the caption underneath the picture:

DIM DIAMOND ASSAULTS MAYOR AND TURNS ON THE LIGHTS

"It must be a misprint," he said.

"Are you sure?" I asked.

Tim sighed – and suddenly he was looking sad. "You know, Nick," he began. "Recently, I've been thinking."

"Did it hurt?" I muttered.

He ignored me. "Maybe I should think about getting another job. I mean, look at me! I'm twenty-eight. I never have any money. I'm six months behind on the rent. I can't remember the last time you and I had a square meal."

"We had pizza the night before last," I reminded him.

"That was circular. And whenever I do get a job – like this business with Miranda – it always seems to go wrong." He sighed again. "She told me I was the most stupid person she'd ever met."

"Maybe she was joking."

"She spat at me and tried to strangle me!"

"Well ... she's Greek."

Tim shook his head. "As soon as the New Year begins, I'm going to find myself a proper job," he said. "It shouldn't be too difficult. I've got qualifications."

I fell silent. I didn't have the heart to remind him that he only had two A levels – and one of them was in embroidery.

It looked as if we were going to have a pretty glum Christmas. But as you'll probably know by now, nothing in our lives ever turns out quite how we expect. A second later there was a knock at the door and before either of us could react, Minerva walked in. I was so surprised, I almost fell off my chair. Tim was so surprised he actually did fall off his.

She was on her own and she was trying to look inconspicuous dressed in jeans and a black jersey with a one-thousand-dollar pair of sunglasses hiding her eyes. But Minerva was Minerva. She couldn't look inconspicuous if she covered herself in mud and sat in a swamp.

"Minerva!" Tim gasped as he picked himself up.

"I didn't want to see you," Minerva said, taking off her sunglasses so she could see him better. "I didn't want to come here," she went on. "But I had to. Last night I behaved like a cow."

"You ate grass?" Tim asked.

"No. I behaved disgracefully towards you. I spat at you. I tried to strangle you. But this morning, when I woke up, I realized I'd got it all wrong." She sat down. "Harold brought in the newspapers and I saw that we got every single front page. And part of that was thanks to you. *The Times* called you a maniac. The *Mail* said you were idiotic. The *Guardian* thought you were a banker."

"That *was* a misprint," I said.

Minerva ignored me. "If I'd just turned on those ridiculous lights, the most I would have got would have been the front page of the evening paper. But the way things turned out, I got more publicity than I could have dreamed of. Harold is certain my new single is going to go straight to number one."

"How is Harold?" I asked.

"He had a very lucky escape last night," Minerva said. "One of those bullets missed him by a centimetre. It even burnt a hole in the side of his coat."

"You mean ... it could have hit his pace-maker?" I exclaimed.

"It was a near miss. But I'm not here to talk about Harold." She turned to Tim. "I want to make it up to you, Timothy," she said. "I want to invite you to dinner. I've already reserved a table for two."

"Isn't two a little early for dinner?" Tim asked.

"For just the two of us, I mean!" Minerva smiled but I wasn't entirely convinced. I'd met sharks with friendlier teeth. "At eight o'clock this evening," she went on. "There's a restaurant I go to. It's called The Gravy." She giggled mischievously. "I thought we might have a little tête-à-tête."

"I'm not that crazy about French food," Tim muttered.

"You'll like this," Minerva simpered. "Make sure you dress up smart. You should put on that suit of yours with seven buttons and seventeen buttonholes."

And with that she was gone.

I went over to the window and looked out as she left the building. There was a police car waiting for her. It was true, then. The men in blue had now taken over Tim's job.

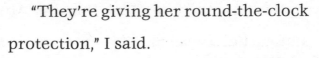

"They're giving her round-the-clock protection," I said.

"They think someone's going to kill her near a clock?"

Tim looked slightly dazed. I could see that he was already imagining himself in some swanky restaurant, drinking champagne with the rich and famous. It was time to bring him down to earth.

"You're not going," I said.

"Why not?" Tim replied.

"She's not interested in you, Tim. If she's invited you out, it's only for the publicity.

That's all she cares about."

"Maybe she's got a soft spot for me."

"I don't think she's got a soft spot for anyone except herself. Anyway, she's a married woman."

"Listen, kid." Tim leant back in his chair. "You don't understand the female mind. Maybe she's looking for something rough and a little bit dangerous."

"Then she can buy herself a yak."

"She likes me!"

"She's using you, Tim."

"She's invited me to dinner!"

"Well, if you're going, I'm going too."

Tim stared at me as if I'd just slapped him in the face – and I can't say I wasn't tempted. "Forget it, Nick," he said. "You heard what she said. This is a dinner for two. I don't need you there. I'm going on my own. And this time, my decision is final!"

The Gravy was one of London's most exclusive restaurants, reserved for celebrities and millionaires. It was so exclusive, even the waiters had trouble getting in, and the name was written in tiny letters as if it didn't want anyone to notice. It was tucked away in a quiet street near Covent Garden with a doorman sizing up everyone who came close. He looked at Tim and me with an expression of complete disgust. But this was the sort of place where even the doormat didn't say **WELCOME**. It preferred to say **GO AWAY**.

Why had I come? Part of the answer was that I was worried about Tim. I still didn't know what Minerva was up to, but I didn't trust her and I wanted to be there if things took a turn for the worse. But also, I quite fancied dinner at The Gravy. The food was said to be so good that the chef actually cried when you ate it. The house speciality was a leg of lamb cooked in Armagnac – and no matter that it cost you an Armagnac and a leg. Even a glass of water at The Gravy was expensive. It probably came out of a gold-plated tap.

The head waiter showed us to the best table, and there was Minerva looking stunning in a white silk dress that hugged her tight in all the right places and tighter still in some of the wrong ones. Her face fell when she saw me but she didn't protest as a couple of waiters hastily added a third setting to the table. It was only as we sat down that she muttered, "I'm surprised you brought your little brother,

Timothy. Couldn't you find a babysitter?"

"I'm no baby, Minerva," I said.

"I was hoping to be alone with your big brother. I want to get to know him a little better."

"Just pretend I'm not here."

And that's exactly what she tried to do for the rest of the meal. The waiter came over with three menus but she chose only for the two of them, leaving me to decide for myself. That suited me. I went for the straightforward steak and chips, leaving the fancy stuff with the French names to her and Tim. If I've got one rule in life, it's never eat anything you can't translate.

"So tell me, Timothy," Minerva said, winking at him. "How would you like a little bubbly?"

Tim looked awkward. "Actually, I had a bath before I came."

"Bollinger!" she exclaimed.

"No. Really. I did!"

Minerva ordered a bottle of Bollinger. I asked for a Coke. The way she was making eyes at Tim, it really did seem that she had designs on him and I couldn't understand it. I mean, he was fifteen years younger than her and about fifty thousand times poorer. What could she see in him? I watched him as he opened the champagne for her. There was an explosive pop, followed by a scream from the other side of the room.

"The head waiter?" Tim asked.

"No," I said. "Just a waiter's head."

Minerva didn't seem to mind. She snuggled up close to him. "I love a man who makes me laugh," she said. "Can I ask you something, Timothy? Do you have a girlfriend?"

"Not at the moment," Tim answered.

"There's nobody waiting for you in bed tonight?"

"It's just Tim and his Paddington Bear hot-water bottle," I told her.

Tim glared at me.

"I fill it for him every night."

The waiter arrived with the first course: soup for me, caviar for Tim and Minerva. Personally, I've never understood caviar. I mean, when I order eggs, I don't expect them to turn up tiny, black and fifty quid a mouthful. But she seemed happy enough. I wondered who would pick up the bill.

I could see that Tim was already well out of his depth. He was looking more and more uncomfortable the closer Minerva got, and she was already close enough. Any closer and she would be on his lap.

"Timothy ... I think you and I were meant for each other," she breathed.

"What about your husband?" Tim squeaked.

She sniffed. "Let's not talk about Harold. He's half the man you are."

"Which half are you talking about?"

I couldn't help chipping in again. "If you dislike him so much," I asked, "why did you marry him?"

To my surprise, Minerva looked me in the eye for the first time and I knew at once that she was going to be completely honest. "Why do you think?" she replied coldly. "I married Harold for his money. That was at the start of my career. I'd just left Athens and I had nothing. He promised to help me – and he did. Of course, all that's changed now. Now I'm worth millions!"

"So why are you still with him?"

"I can't be bothered to divorce him. Anyway, it's more fun the way things are."

"Does he know where you are tonight?"

Minerva laughed. "Of course he knows. You should have seen his face when I told him I was going out with Timothy. I thought he was going to have a heart attack!"

So that was why she had invited Tim to The Gravy. I should have seen it from the start. Minerva loathed her husband – that much had been obvious when we first met them at their suite at the hotel – and she amused herself by humiliating him. And what better way than to be seen out in public with someone like my big brother, Tim?

At that moment I disliked her as much as anyone I had ever known. More than Charon, the four-fingered assassin we met in Amsterdam. More than my homicidal French teacher, Monsieur Palis. The thing about Minerva was that she was beautiful, rich and loved by millions. But she had the heart of a snake.

Somehow we got through to the next course. My steak was fine but I didn't like the look of the grey, jelly-like dish that Minerva had ordered for herself and Tim. It came in a yellow sauce with rice and beans.

Tim wasn't sure either. He had eaten about half of it when he stopped and looked up. "What did you say this was?" he asked.

"Cervelles de veaux au beurre."

He took another mouthful. "It tastes interesting," he said. "What does that mean?"

"Grilled calves' brains in butter."

Two minutes later we were standing outside on the pavement with the doorman glowering at us, glad to see us go.

"That was a nice evening," I said.

"Do you think Minerva enjoyed it?" Tim asked.

"Well, you may have spoiled it a bit when you were sick on her." I looked around for a bus or a taxi.

"I want to go home," Tim groaned. He was still looking very green.

"To Paddington Bear?"

"Just get us a cab!"

But as it turned out, we weren't going to need a bus or a cab. Because just then a car came screeching to a halt in front of us and two men leapt out.

"IT'S A POLICE CAR!" Tim exclaimed.

That was particularly brilliant of him and I wasn't sure how he'd worked it out.

Maybe it was the blue uniforms the men were wearing. Or it could have been the car with its flashing lights and the word **POLICE** emblazoned on the side. But he was right. I thought they'd come to look after Minerva – but it was the two of us they made for.

"Are you Tim Diamond?" one of them asked.

"Yes..."

"Get in the car. You're coming down to the station."

"What's going on?" I demanded. "What's happened? And how did you know we were here?"

They ignored me.

The policeman was examining Tim. "We want to talk to you," he said.

"What about?" Tim quavered.

The policeman smiled but without a shred of warmth or humour. It was the sort of smile a doctor might give you before he explained you only had a week to live. "You're wanted, Mr Diamond," he said. "For murder."

The Dead Man

I don't like police stations. They're full of violent and dangerous characters who need to be kept away from modern society ... and I'm not talking about the crooks. A lot of people say the British police are wonderful, but I'd have to disagree. I was only fourteen but I had been arrested so often, it couldn't be long before they gave me my own set of personalized handcuffs. I even spent a month in prison once – and I hadn't done anything wrong! When I look back on it, there's only one word to describe the way I've been treated. Criminal.

This time they drove us to a police station in Holborn, about ten minutes' drive from The Gravy. Tim had gone very pale and quiet in the back of the car. *Cervelles de veaux au beurre* and now this! We stopped and the two policemen led us in through a door and down the usual corridor with white tiles on the walls and hard neon lighting above ... the sort of corridor that can only take you somewhere you don't want to be. There was an interrogation room at the end: four chairs, one table and two detectives. The furniture was hard and unattractive but that was nothing compared to the men.

Detective Chief Inspector Snape and

Detective Superintendent Boyle. They were old friends and, like most of Tim's old friends, they hated us. Why was it that whenever we got into trouble, the two of them always seemed to show up? Surely the Metropolitan Police could have found two new officers to molest us? Anyway, put an ape and a Rottweiler in suits and you'll get a rough idea of Snape and Boyle. Snape was the older of the two and the one less likely to have rabies. He was looking old, I thought. But he'd probably looked old the day he was born.

"Well, this really is the perfect end to a horrible day," Snape began as we sat down. It didn't look as if he was going to offer us a cup of tea. "Tim Diamond! The only detective in London with no brains."

Tim went a little green.

"I wouldn't mention brains unless you know a good dry cleaner," I said.

"I want to go to bed!" Tim moaned.

"You're not going anywhere, Diamond," Snape cut in. "I'm investigating a murder and right now you're my only suspect."

"Can I hit him?" Boyle asked hopefully.

"No, Boyle."

"Can I hit his little brother?"

"No!"

"But they were resisting arrest, sir!"

"We haven't arrested them yet, Boyle." Snape shook his head and sighed. "I've just sent Boyle on an anger-management course," he told us.

"Did it work?" I asked.

"No. He got angry and hit the manager so they sent him back again."

"Well you're wasting your time," I said. "We haven't murdered anyone."

Snape looked at me with disdain. "What can you tell me about a man called Reginald Parker?" he said.

"I can't tell you anything, Snape," I said. "We've never met him."

"What's happened to him?" Tim asked.

"He's been murdered," Snape replied. "He was strangled this afternoon. He lived at 27 Sparrow Lane and his neighbour heard the sound of a fight. She called us and we found the body."

"What makes you think it's got anything to do with us?" I asked.

Snape nodded at Boyle. "Show them!"

Boyle leant down and produced a car battery connected to a tangle of wires with clamps on the end. He placed it on the table and glanced unpleasantly at Tim. Snape raised his eyes. "I don't mean that! I want you to show them the evidence!"

Boyle scowled. He opened a drawer and this time he produced a transparent evidence bag with something inside it. I recognized it at once. **NO PROBLEM TOO PROBLEMATIC**. It was Tim's business card.

"We found this next to the body," Snape said. "How do you explain that?"

"A coincidence?" Tim suggested.

Snape's face darkened. "Of course it's not a coincidence, you idiot! It's a clue! Was Reginald Parker a client of yours? That wouldn't surprise me. Anyone stupid enough to hire you would almost certainly wind up dead."

I shook my head. "I told you, Chief Inspector. We've never seen him."

"How can you be so sure of that? I haven't even told you what he looked like."

Boyle opened the drawer a second time and produced a black and white photograph.

You can always tell when the police have taken a picture of someone after they're dead. They don't smile for the camera. In fact, they don't do anything. And the black and the white somehow seems to suit them. All the colour has already gone. The photograph showed a short, plump man with curly hair, lying on his back in the mess that had once been the room where he lived. I gasped. Because the truth was that I did know him. I had seen him once and only briefly, but it wasn't a face I was going to forget.

Reginald Parker was the man who had tried to shoot Minerva. He was the man on the roof above Regent Street.

"Did you find a gun in his room?" I asked.

Snape shook his head. "No. I told you. He was strangled."

"How about a handful of silver acorns? Or anything to do with oak trees?"

Boyle leant over the table and grabbed me by the collar. I felt myself being dragged to

my feet. My feet left the floor. One of my shirt buttons went shooting over my shoulder. "Are you taking the mickey?" he demanded.

"No!" I gurgled. "I'm trying to help you. I did meet this man. I just didn't know his name."

Boyle turned to Snape, still holding me in the air. "Shall I wire him up to the car battery, sir?"

"Certainly not, Boyle!" Snape looked offended. "He's going to tell us everything anyway."

"I know that, sir. But this way he'll tell us quicker."

"Just put him down!"

Boyle looked on the edge of tears but he dropped me back into my seat. And then I told them everything that had happened since Jake Hammill had walked into our office. The meeting at the hotel. The events in Regent Street. Snape nodded when I talked about that. He must have seen Tim on the news.

"You're sure it was Parker on the roof?" he asked.

"It's the same face, Chief Inspector," I said.

"And you think he was a member of this organization – Overweight Albanian Kids?"

"He was certainly overweight." I nodded at the photograph.

"But as far as we know, he wasn't Albanian."

"Maybe he lived in Albania when he was young."

"We'll check it out."

"Does this mean you're letting us go?" Tim asked, getting to his feet.

"Not so fast, Diamond!"

"All right." Tim sat down, then got up more slowly.

Snape glowered. "I'll see you two again!" he said.

"Yeah. And I'll be waiting." Boyle was standing there holding one of the electrical contacts in his hand. The other was on the table. I passed it to him.

"Don't forget this," I said.

He took it in the other hand.

We could still hear Boyle screaming as we raced back down the corridor and out onto the street. But that's the modern police for you. Shocking.

When Tim and I had breakfast the next morning, I could see he was deep in thought.

He didn't even react when he upturned the cereal packet and got the plastic toy.

"I just don't get it," he said at length.

"What's that, Tim?"

"Well ... this guy ... Archibald Porter."

"I think you mean Reginald Parker."

"He tried to kill Minerva and now somebody has killed him. But that doesn't make any sense. Nobody knew who he was. So why kill him? If they wanted to protect Minerva, they could have just reported him to the police."

He frowned but then his eyes brightened. "Maybe it was just another coincidence!" he exclaimed. "Maybe his death was an accident!"

"It's quite tricky to get strangled by accident," I pointed out.

Tim nodded. "I wonder how he got my business card?"

"That's exactly what we're going to find out..."

We were lucky that Snape had given us Parker's address. As soon as Tim had finished breakfast, we looked up Sparrow Lane in Tim's *A–Z*. Actually, it was an *A–W*. He'd got it cheap. Then we took a bus to the other side of London and a narrow street of terraced houses not far from the old meat market. Number 27 was halfway down and looked exactly the same as numbers 25 and 29 – apart, that is, from the policeman on duty and the blue and white POLICE LINE: DO NOT CROSS taped over the front door.

To be honest, I'd forgotten that Snape would have left someone on duty and I could see at a glance that we weren't going to get past the policeman at the door. He had the sort of face that if he ever decided to join the dog unit, he wouldn't need a dog. Ignoring him, I went straight to the house next door and rang the bell, hoping the owner would be in.

She was. The door opened and a huge, cheerful Caribbean woman in a brilliantly coloured dress appeared on the doorstep, the great slabs that were arms folded across her ample breast. "Yes, me darlings? How can I help you?" she boomed out.

I nudged Tim.

"I'm Tim Diamond," Tim said.

"Yes?" The woman was none the wiser.

"My brother is a private detective," I told her. "He wants to ask you some questions about the guy who lived next door."

"That's right," Tim explained. "And if he

lived next door, then I'd imagine he must have been your neighbour."

"That's brilliant, Tim," I muttered. "How did you work that one out?"

It turned out that the woman was called Mrs Winterbotham and had lived at number 25 for almost as many years. Her husband was out, working at the meat market, and she invited us into her kitchen and gave us tea and coconut biscuits. She had already told the police everything but she was going to enjoy telling us again.

"Reginald was an actor," she said, then looked left and right and lowered her voice as if he might be listening from beyond the grave. "But he wasn't a very good one. Oh no! He was out of work most of the time. He was in *The Cherry Orchard* last May, playing one of the cherries. And last year he appeared at the Unicorn Theatre in a one-man show."

"Was it popular?" I asked.

"No. Only one man came." Mrs Winterbotham dropped three sugar cubes into her tea and helped herself to another biscuit. "Reginald was a nice man. But, you know, I'm not sure it really helped his career, his having a stutter."

I remembered now. Parker had stuttered when he was on the roof. So it hadn't been because he was afraid.

"I said to him that he ought to be a mime artist," Mrs Winterbotham went on. "That way he wouldn't have had to talk. But I don't think people would have paid to see him. He didn't have the figure for it. To be honest with you, I've seen more attractive figures hanging up in the meat market."

"When was his last job?" I asked.

"Well..." She put down the biscuit and leant forward conspiratorially. "That's what I told the police. He always got a job at Christmas. He worked in a department store. But this year something very unusual happened. He got paid for a one-night appearance in the West End! He didn't tell me what it was but I do know that it was a lot of money."

"Who paid him?"

"He never said. But I don't think it can have worked out because when I saw him the next morning, he was very upset."

"How do you know he was upset?" Tim asked.

"He was crying."

"You're sure they weren't tears of happiness?"

"Oh no, Mr Diamond. He was completely miserable. And then that afternoon, someone came to the house. I heard this banging and crashing and I went round to the garden to see what was happening. Then there was silence. I knocked on the door but I got no answer. So I called the police."

"Just one last question, Mrs Winterbotham..." I began.

"Please. Call me Janey!"

"Was Reginald Parker Albanian?"

"No. As far as I know, he'd never been to Albania. In fact, he never went anywhere. He couldn't afford it. Most of the time he just sat at home and watched TV." She sighed and I got the idea that maybe she'd been his only friend in the world. "And now he's dead. I can't believe it. Now, how about a nice piece of banana cake?"

We didn't have the cake.

Because suddenly, even as Mrs Winterbotham had been talking, everything had made sense. Suddenly I was back on the roof, hearing Reginald Parker as he called out across the gap. *I d-d-didn't...* I saw the cracker with the acorn and the death threat and knew what it was that was wrong with the letter Minerva had been sent. I thought about Regent Street and the bullet that had come so close it had drilled a hole in Harold Chase's coat. I knew exactly what job Reginald had been hired for – it could only be one job – and I also knew what was going to happen at twelve o'clock that day. I looked at my watch. It was five past eleven. We had less than one hour left.

"We have to get to Harrods, Tim!" I said.

Tim shook his head. "This is no time for Christmas shopping, Nick."

"We're not going shopping. We have to find Minerva."

"Why?"

A taxi drove by. I reached out and flagged it down.

"She's going to be murdered, Tim. And I know who by."

Killer with a Smile

We were on the wrong side of town. We had to cross the whole of London to reach Knightsbridge, and with Christmas just weeks away the traffic could hardly be worse. As we sat in a traffic jam on the edge of Hyde Park I could feel the minutes ticking away. Worse than that, I could see them. The taxi meter was running and Tim was staring at it in dismay, watching as the last of his earnings disappeared.

We finally made it with about five minutes and ten pounds to spare, but even so it was going to be tight. Harrods was a huge place and the grotto was right up on the fourth floor. Worse than that, the entire store was heaving – not just with shoppers but with the usual crowd of fans and policemen who had turned out to see or to protect Minerva. There were security men on all the doors and more photographers waiting in the street, although you'd have thought by now the papers would have had enough of her. I certainly had.

And what nobody knew was that the killer was already inside the building. He would smile at Minerva and he would murder her ... and she wouldn't even know it had happened until she woke up dead.

"This way, Tim!"

We had plunged off the street and into women's handbags, then into cosmetics, then food. Harrods was every Christmas present you could ever imagine – more presents than anyone in the world could ever want. It was Christmas gone mad: hundreds of miles of tinsel; thousands of glittering stars and balls; enough Christmas trees to repopulate a forest. Don't get me wrong. I love Christmas and I'll tear open as many presents as I can get my hands on. But as I ran for the escalators, past the groaning shelves and the grinning sales assistants, I couldn't help but feel there had to be something more to it than this. Maybe something less, if you know what I mean.

We reached the escalators and began to fight our way up. I had a strange sense of déjà vu as I went. Suddenly I was in another department store in a different part of London almost two years before. I'd been running then too – to escape from two German assassins who'd been trying to make sure that the only way I saw Boxing Day was from inside a box. But that was another time and another story and if you want to know about it, I'm afraid you're going to have to buy another book.

We got to the fourth floor and there was a sign pointing towards Santa's grotto, "Jingle Bells" blaring out of the speakers and little kids everywhere, dragging their mothers to see the man in red.

I stopped, panting. "I hope we're not too late," I gasped.

"Yes," Tim agreed. "Santa may not have any presents left!"

Sometimes I think Tim doesn't belong in the real world. Maybe he'd be more comfortable in a nice white room with padded walls. But this was no time to argue. It was twelve noon exactly. Somewhere in the clock department down below, a thousand clocks would be chiming, bleeping or shooting out cuckoos. The grotto had just been opened by Minerva. And the way ahead was blocked.

There were toys everywhere. Vast Lego castles, cuddly toys, jigsaw mountains and Scalextric cars buzzing round in furious circles. Children were pulling and pushing in every direction. In the far distance I could see the green, plastic entrance to a green, plastic cave with a long line of people waiting to go in. That was where we had to be. But our path had been closed off by a sixteen-stone store security guard with the body of a wrestler and the face of a boxer at the end of a particularly vicious fight. At least, I assumed he was a security guard. It was hard to be sure. He was dressed as an elf.

"You can't go this way!" he told me. "You have to go to the back of the queue." So he *was* a security guard. I should have known. How many elves do you see carrying truncheons?

"Where's Minerva?" I demanded. I was afraid I was already too late – and this brute in green tights was only making things worse.

"She's in with Santa Claus, opening the grotto. You'll have to wait in line if you want her autograph."

"I don't want her autograph. I want to save her life!"

But it was no good. I might as well have

argued with Rudolph the Red-Nosed Reindeer (there was a mechanical version next to the cave). I had to stop myself pulling out my hair. I was expecting a gunshot at any moment and here I was trying to reason with an elf. I looked around me, wondering if I could bribe him with a cuddly toy – or if not, hit him with one. That was when I saw Detective Chief Inspector Snape, standing grim-faced with Boyle next to him, the two of them surrounded by Barbie dolls.

"SNAPE!" I shouted out, and before the security guard could stop me I had run over to the two men.

"What are you doing here, Diamond?" he snapped the moment he saw me.

Boyle curled his lip and looked ugly – which in his case wasn't very difficult. Once again he lumbered forward and grabbed hold of me.

"Don't worry, Boyle!" I said. "I haven't come here to steal your Barbie doll."

"Then why are you here?" Snape demanded.

"You've got to find Minerva," I began. "She's in danger."

"I know she's in danger," Snape replied. "Boyle and I are on special duty. We're looking after her."

"You don't understand..."

How could I tell them what I knew? There wasn't enough time and with all the noise in the place – the children screaming, the music playing, Rudolph singing and all the rest of it – I'd have been hoarse before I got to the end. But just then Minerva appeared, coming out of the grotto with her manager, Jake Hammill, next to her. There was no sign of her husband, but somehow I wasn't surprised.

I twisted out of Boyle's grip, and with Tim right behind me I ran over to her. As usual, Minerva was looking drop-dead gorgeous in a slinky, silver number, and despite everything I was glad that I had arrived in time and that she hadn't, after all, dropped dead. She was holding a present, about the size and shape of a shoe box. Santa must have just given it to her.

She saw me. **"YOU!"** she snapped – and unless that's Greek for Happy Christmas, she wasn't too pleased to see me.

I stood in front of her, my eyes fixed on the box. I didn't want to touch it. To be honest, I didn't want to be anywhere near it.

I had a good idea what was inside.

"Did Santa give you that?" I demanded.

"Yes." She nodded.

"Do you know what it is?"

Minerva shrugged. She didn't really care. She was only here for the publicity. "No," she said.

"I think it's a clock," Tim chimed in.

"Why?"

"Well ... I can hear it ticking."

Snape leant forward and took the box. "What's all this about?" he demanded.

"Chief Inspector," I said, and suddenly my mouth was dry. "I'd be very careful with that unless you want to spend this Christmas in six different parts of London all at the same time."

"What are you talking about?" Hammill demanded.

"There's probably an oak leaf or two in there and maybe some acorns. But I'll bet you any money that the rest of it is a bomb."

Maybe I said the word too loudly. Somehow the crowd caught on to what was happening and suddenly the entire department was filled with hysterical mothers dragging their screaming kids off to the nearest escalator. I ignored them. I just wanted to know if Snape was going to believe me. And to be fair to him, just this once he gave me the benefit of the doubt. Very gently, he lowered the box to the ground, then turned to Boyle. "Have you got a knife?" he asked.

Boyle reached into his pocket and took out first a cut-throat razor, then a bayonet and finally a flick knife. He pressed a button and ten centimetres of ugly steel leapt out to join in the cheerful Christmas atmosphere. Snape took it. Very carefully, he cut a square in the side of the parcel and peeled the cardboard back. He looked inside.

"He's right!" he said.

He didn't need to tell me. Looking over his shoulder, I could just make out part of an alarm clock, some loops of wire and something that could have been Plasticine but definitely wasn't.

Snape looked up. "Plastic explosive," he whispered. "It's connected to an alarm clock. It'll blow up when the bell goes." He squinted through the square he had cut out. Then, very slowly, he handed the package to Boyle. "All right, Boyle," he said. "This is timed to go off in forty minutes. You'd better get it down to the bomb disposal squad."

"Where's that?" I asked.

"It's a forty-five-minute drive away."

Boyle stared at him.

"See if you can find a short cut," Snape advised.

Boyle disappeared – in a hurry. Snape turned to me. "So what's this all about?" he demanded.

"Santa just gave me that!" Minerva rasped. She was standing there dazed.

"Have you been a bad girl this year?" Tim asked.

"It's not Santa!" I said. "Come on..."

The five of us – me, Tim, Minerva, Jake Hammill and Snape – dived into the grotto. Out of the corner of my eye I saw the security guard talking into his radio, presumably calling for reinforcements. There was nobody else left on the fourth floor – as far as I knew, there was nobody left in Knightsbridge. White plastic snow crunched underfoot as we followed the path into the cave. White plastic stalactites hung down and white plastic stalagmites pointed up – or maybe it was the other way round. I can never remember. We passed a couple more mechanical singing reindeer and arrived just in time to see a familiar red figure, about to leave by a back exit.

"HOLD IT RIGHT THERE, SANTA!" I shouted.

Santa froze, then slowly turned around.

"It's ... it's ... it's...!" Tim exclaimed. He stopped. He had no idea who it was, and with the red hood, the white beard and the golden-framed spectacles, I couldn't blame him. His own mother wouldn't recognize him. His own wife hadn't.

I walked forward and pulled off the beard. And there he was.

"HAROLD!" Minerva exclaimed.

"Harold?" Hammill quavered.

"That's right," I said. "Harold Chase."

There could be no doubt about it. The old man reached up and lowered the hood, revealing more of his face, his silver hair and his hearing aid. He had concealed his permanent suntan with make-up. But there could be no disguising the venom with which he was looking at his wife.

Snape took over. "You just gave Minerva a bomb," he said.

Harold Chase said nothing.

"That's a very original present," Tim commented.

"Not really, Tim," I said. "He was trying to kill her."

It was the word "kill" that did it. The bomb

had been taken away. But Harold Chase exploded. **"I HATE HER!"** he screamed. "You have no idea what it's been like living with her! I know why she married me. **SHE WANTED MY MONEY!** But now that she's so big and so famous she doesn't need me. And so she humiliates and belittles me. **SHE'S MADE MY LIFE HELL!"**

He took a step towards us. Tim took three steps back.

"But that's not the worst of it," Harold went on. "She's a hypocrite. She smiles at the crowds on Regent Street when secretly she despises them. She hates Christmas too – and every year she's ruined it for me. No carols, no presents, no tinsel, no fun. She's stolen Christmas from me and that was a good enough reason to want to see her dead."

By now, he was frothing at the mouth and I almost wished Boyle was there to deal with him. Fortunately the security guard disguised as an elf had appeared with two colleagues, and the three of them dragged Harold out. He was still screaming as he went.

The five of us went back downstairs to a champagne bar on the ground floor. It was somewhere quiet and we had a lot to talk about. Minerva paid for champagne for herself and the others. I got a glass of lemonade. I had to admit she seemed very shaken by what had happened. Her face was pale. Her eyes were thoughtful. And even her silver-plated breasts seemed to have lost their sparkle.

"All right, Diamond," Snape said, empty-ing his glass. "Spit it out!"

"He hasn't drunk anything yet," Tim said.

"I want you to tell me what's been going on. How did you know about Harold Chase and how did you figure out his plan?"

"I worked it out when we visited Janey Winterbotham," I explained.

"The next-door neighbour?" Snape sniffed. "I spoke to her. She didn't tell me anything."

"She told me that Reginald Parker was an out-of-work actor but that he had a job in a department store every Christmas," I said. "What else could he have been but a depart-ment store Santa? That was when it all fell into place."

"Why don't you start at the beginning?" Jake Hammill suggested.

"All right." I drew a breath. "This is the way I see it. Harold Chase hated Minerva for all the reasons he just told us. His hatred had obviously driven him mad and he decided to kill her. But the trouble was, it was too obvious. If Minerva died, he would be the main suspect. Everyone knew how badly she treated him."

"A lot of people would die to be married to me," Minerva sniffed.

"He was married to you – and you were the one he wanted to die," I reminded her. "Anyway, Harold couldn't kill you himself. He'd be arrested at once. But then he had an idea. He realized that the best way to get rid of you was to create someone who didn't exist: a crazy fan. He used that concert you cancelled – for Overweight Albanian Kids – and pretended that someone was out to get revenge."

"You mean ... it was Harold who wrote that anonymous letter?" Hammill asked.

"Exactly. He even put a fake spelling mistake in it – but if he couldn't spell 'forgive', how come he could spell 'forget' a few lines later? The whole thing felt fake to me."

"And what about the cracker?"

 "That was another clue. I thought at the time that there was something weird about it, but it was only later that I realized what it was." I turned to Hammill. "You'd booked Minerva into the Porchester hotel under a false name."

"Right," he said.

"But the box of crackers was addressed to her. Whoever sent it even knew the number of the suite where she was staying. It had to be an inside job."

"But wait a minute," Snape interrupted. "If it was Chase all the time, what was Reginald Parker doing on the roof at Regent Street?"

"Reginald Parker had been paid by Chase," I explained. "His neighbour told us he got a lot of money for a job in the West End. She probably thought it was a job in theatre. My guess is that Chase paid him to leave the silver oak leaves on the roof. Parker had no idea what he was doing. He didn't have a gun or anything. I saw him carrying something, but it could have been a camera. After all, he knew Minerva was there. He was a complete innocent. That's what he tried to tell me when I went up there. 'I didn't...' That was all he managed. But what he wanted to say was, 'I didn't do it!' He must have been horrified when he heard the shots."

"So who did shoot at me?" Minerva asked. She poured herself some more champagne. I wondered what she was celebrating. Maybe it was the fact she was still alive.

"That was Harold," I said. "Again, I'm only guessing, but I'd say he fired two blank shots from a gun he had inside his pocket. When we were on the platform, the shots sounded very close. He fired twice and then pointed to Reginald up on the roof – because, of course, he knew he'd be there. You see, he was creating the illusion of a killer ... someone who didn't really exist. The only snag is, the gun burnt a hole in his coat." I glanced at Minerva. "You thought he'd almost been hit.

In fact, he'd fired the shots himself."

"I don't get it," Minerva exclaimed. "He wanted to protect me! It was Harold who persuaded me to get a bodyguard!"

"He did that to throw off any suspicion. At the same time, he made sure you hired the worst private detective in London. Someone too stupid to get in the way of his plan."

"And who was that?" Tim asked.

"Have some more champagne, Tim," I said.

"And then Harold Chase killed Reginald Parker," Snape said.

"You've got it in one, Chief Inspector. Chase had chosen Parker because he knew he was going to be the Santa Claus at Harrods. First of all he hired him to go on the roof. Then he killed him and took his place. Tim's business card must have fallen out of his pocket during the fight. It was when I saw the card that I put two and two together..."

"You did your maths homework?" Tim asked.

"No, Tim. I cracked the case."

There was a long silence. Either I'd been talking too slowly or they'd been drinking too quickly but all the champagne was gone. And I hadn't even touched my lemonade.

Jake Hammill put an arm around Minerva. "Baby, I'm so sorry," he said. "What a terrible experience for you!"

Minerva shrugged. "It wasn't so bad," she said. "I've got rid of Harold. I'm going to get lots of publicity. And my single is certain to go to number one." She got to her feet. I thought she was going to leave, but she took one last look at me. "You're quite smart for a scruffy fourteen-year-old," she said. Then she flicked her eyes towards Tim. "As for you, you're just an utter loss."

She walked out.

"What did she mean?" Tim wailed.

I thought for a moment. "Justanutterloss. It's Greek for sensational," I said.

"Really?" Tim's eyes lit up.

"Sure, Tim," I said. Well, after all, it was Christmas.

There are a few things to add.

Two weeks later, Tim and I got a surprise in the post – and this time it wasn't a bomb, an unpaid bill or a poison pen letter. It was a note from Jake Hammill. It seemed that he wasn't so bad after all. We had just saved his most famous client from a murder attempt that would have been not only the end of her career, but – even worse – the end of his percentage. And as a token of his gratitude, he'd decided to send us a cheque for ten thousand pounds. I'll never forget the sight of Tim holding it between his hands. The last time he had seen that many zeros, it had been in his school report.

We talked a lot about what to do with the money. Of course, we were going to have a proper Christmas lunch. Tim was going to pay off the rent. I was finally going to get a new school uniform – the last one had so many patches in it, it was more patches than uniform. But that would still leave us with several thousand pounds, which was just about the most money we'd ever had.

I forget who suggested it first, but that

was when we decided to fly out to Australia to be reunited with our parents. It had been years since we'd seen them, and sometimes I thought it was unnatural for a young lad to be living without his mother, often crying himself to sleep, having to be tucked in every night and cheered up by his brother. Not that I minded doing all that for Tim, but even so I thought it would do us all good to be a family again, just for a while.

And the next day we bought two British Airways tickets to Sydney. We were going to travel out as soon as the Easter term ended, and maybe one day I'll write down what actually happened when we got there. *The Radius of the Lost Shark*. That's the title I've got written down in my notebook. It's another story I've got to tell.

What else is there? Harold Chase got life in jail for attempted murder, but looking at him I didn't think that would be too many years. Snape took the credit for the arrest, of course. They actually put his face on the front cover of the monthly police journal, *Hello, Hello, Hello* magazine. Reginald Parker's remains were scattered in the River Thames, in front of the National Theatre – as he'd requested in his will. It can't have been pleasant, though. He hadn't been cremated.

And what about Minerva? She may have got to number one, but I didn't care. I never listened to her music again. She may have had everything, but without a heart you're just nothing. She was like a December without Christmas – and at the end of the day, what's the point of that?

Anthony Horowitz is the author of the number one bestselling Alex Rider books and The Power of Five series. He has enjoyed huge success as a writer for both children and adults, most recently with the latest adventure in the Alex Rider series, *Russian Roulette* and the highly acclaimed Sherlock Holmes novels, *The House of Silk* and *Moriarty*. Anthony was also chosen by the Ian Fleming estate to write the new James Bond novel, *Trigger Mortis*, which was published in September 2015. Anthony has won numerous awards, including the Bookseller Association/Nielsen Author of the Year Award, the Children's Book of the Year Award at the British Book Awards, and the Red House Children's Book Award. In 2014 Anthony was awarded an OBE for Services to Literature. He has also created and written many major television series, including *Injustice*, *Collision* and the award-winning *Foyle's War*.

You can find out more about Anthony and his work at:
www.anthonyhorowitz.com